GW00776696

Omzak

The Space Cat Warrior

Omzak

The Space Cat warrior

Jaylen Grace

Wishing you the very best

Jaylen Grace

Book Guild Publishing
Sussex, England

First published in Great Britain in 2012 by
The Book Guild Ltd
Pavilion View
19 New Road
Brighton, BN1 1UF

Copyright © Jaylen Grace 2012
Illustrations by Almuth Scheller
www.omzak.co

Typesetting in Palatino by
Nat-Type, Cheshire

Printed in Great Britain by
CPI Group (UK) Ltd, Croydon, CR0 4YY

A catalogue record for this book is available from
The British Library.

ISBN 978 1 84624 796 5

1

Hasty exit from Catopia

CLACK. CLACK.

'How many more times do I need to tell you –
hold your stick across your chest,' I said. 'Swing it in
an arc. Step forward.'

CLACK.

'Keep some distance between your back paws.'

CLACK.

'Try to block me.'

There was the crack of bamboo hitting leather as I struck Romi's chest plate. He winced at the blow.

'Use your stick with force,' I instructed.

CLOP.

'Thrust it at my throat.'

I let Romi get near, knocked the stick from his paws and wedged it under his armpit. I wasn't used to teaching an amateur. It was testing my patience to the core. 'In real combat, I'd have broken your arm,' I said.

Romi loosened his body armour and blew down it. 'Phoo, this is hot work, Captain Omzak.'

He was pouring with sweat. It was even dripping off his tail. 'Stop complaining,' I said. 'Next technique.' I clasped the bamboo pole with both front paws. 'To prepare: imagine you're a golfer finishing his swing.' I swung the stick to shoulder level. 'Then, bring it over your opponent's head and *strike*.' I showed him how, stopping short of his skull so I didn't crack it open. 'Your turn.'

Romi charged, swung his stick, but didn't block my counter strike fast enough. His stick skittered away across the floor. 'I'll get this right in a minute,' he said, chasing after it.

I looked around and let out a sigh. *I, an undefeated warrior, have been reduced to giving secret lessons in the changing area,* I thought. *And doing kitchen duties.*

My ears pricked up. 'Someone's coming. If anyone sees me, I'm in for it.' We jumped into a shower cubicle and I pulled the curtain across.

There was a sound of squeaking metal as someone opened then closed a locker. 'Let's get back to it,' I said once I was sure they had left, 'before anyone else comes in.'

Romi had stuck his tongue out under the showerhead to catch the drips. 'I'm too tired. Could you show me that tail technique again, so I can practise at home?'

'*Too tired?* You'd be useless on a battlefield!' I picked up Romi's stick, then mine. 'This is the *last* time I'm showing you.' I twirled both sticks up into the air, spun on the tip of my tail, closed my eyes and caught them.

'You're astounding, Captain Omzak! Can I have another lesson tomorrow?'

I smoothed my fur down. 'Deal,' I said. I didn't have much choice. He was emptying rubbish bins in return.

'I think it's a brilliant swap that I get to have you as my teacher,' Romi said, unbuckling his body shield. 'But I still think our ruler is mean, giving you kitchen duties as a punishment. If he hated germs as much as you do, I bet *he* wouldn't do it.'

3

'He considered my crime deserved it – to teach me a lesson.' I twirled my whiskers to stay calm.

'What was your crime?' Romi asked, splashing water on his face.

'I saw a Varian clumping over the boundary line into our territory, lost my temper and got in a fight,' I said, pulling on my military jacket.

'I'm sure he deserved it,' Romi said, looking at me in admiration. 'You know what, you're the spitting image of one of the warriors in the hall of fame. You've got the same pure white fur, electric-blue eyes and big whiskers.'

'I bet he never got kitchen duties!' I tugged my jacket down.

'Have you got to get back there?' asked Romi.

'Back to the *nightmare* – yes.'

I went to the kitchen with a heavy heart. The chef – a dumpy Catopian who grinned non-stop – was holding out a plate. 'In appreciation for giving me karate lessons,' he said.

'You turn a blind eye when Romi stands in for me. It's the least I can do.'

'Hope you like it,' he grinned, lifting the cover. *Oh no, runny egg is splattered all over the salmon.* My whiskers shot out like they'd been electrocuted. 'Get it away, before I throw up!'

'Oh – I forgot.' The chef rocked his head in his paws. 'You hate it when different food types touch.'

'Wasn't hungry anyway,' I lied.

I pulled a white coat on over my jacket, pushed my paws in rubber gloves and marched to the sink. It was stacked with dirty dishes. The water looked scummy. Bits of food floated on top. I inched out a plate covered in greasy globs. *There have to be a million germs crawling about.* My fur itched. My skin prickled.

'OMZAK!' Leorio's voice boomed out. The plate slipped out of my paws. A wave of bubbles went up my nose. 'Yes, sir?'

'I want to see you in my chambers. NOW!'

Someone has told on me. The ruler has found out about my swap system.

'Yes, sir,' I said, saluting.

The minute I saw Leorio, the ruler of Catopia, I knew things weren't good. Normally, he would have been sitting cross-legged on his platform. Now he was pacing up and down, his robe swishing, his tail thumping like a hammer.

'You've become a sneaky, unmanageable teenager.' Leorio dragged his claws through the ruff of copper fur around his neck. 'As well as a show off – who thinks he's best at everything.'

'With respect, sir, I don't *think* I'm the best. I am the best. I have a shelf of trophies to prove it.' I gave my whiskers an indignant tug.

'You're arrogant,' Leorio said. 'Who else would

have the nerve to bribe someone to wash out bins?' He walked to the end of his chamber, stood at the glass-panelled wall and stared out at the desert. He was so enraged his chest was going in and out like an accordion.

I thought back to the fight at the boundary line that had got me in trouble in the first place. Leorio hadn't talked to me since then. I needed to be bold and justify my actions.

'I know I should have backed off when I saw Skabbart, but he's a scumbag and deserved what was coming. Not only because of what he did on Planet Fos but because…'

Leorio glared at me. 'SHUT UP, Omzak. We signed a peace treaty with the Varians and Skabbart's a Varian.'

'That ape-bodied creature! Skabbart shouldn't have even crossed our boundary line. Varians are supposed to stay on their own side.'

'I *KNOW* that,' he said. 'But it's still our responsibility to hand trespassers over and let their own kind deal with them – which was my intention before *you* stuck your nose in.'

Leorio jabbed the medals on my jacket. 'You may be Catopia's youngest warrior, national champion of martial arts and whatever else, but your medals count for nothing when you set such a bad example.' He waved a paw. 'Take it off.'

I stood there, dumbstruck. Ordering me to take my jacket off was *mega* serious.

'NOW,' Leorio bellowed.

I fumbled with the buttons, trying to get them undone.

'And what other Catopian puts so much starch in his jacket that it takes an hour to get off?'

Leorio tossed my jacket on his platform and went quiet. He plumped up a cushion for what felt like a week.

BOOF, CRASH, BANG! A meteorite collision turned the sky bright orange. Chunks of rock and metal smacked against the glass pane. I was used to such sights but my tail still stood up like a poker. Leorio's silence was making me nervous. My heart was banging against my ribs.

'I'm sending you to England,' Leorio said.

'Where?' I reeled back in shock, tripped over my tail and crashed to the floor like a sack of nails. 'You can't mean *England*, on Planet Earth?' I said, looking up.

'You heard correctly,' Leorio said.

Trying to stay calm, I pulled myself up. 'Why?'

'So you can live amongst Earth cats, experience life as someone's pet, shake off your arrogance – and look for ways to make up for what you've done!'

'But Earth cats can't speak, they meow – they walk on all fours,' I protested.

'You learned the language of our ancestors in nursery school,' Leorio sniffed. 'And walking on all fours will remind you of your roots.'

I flopped back down. *I'm a space cat warrior. This can't be happening.*

'I'm much bigger than an Earth cat, won't I look out of place?' I gulped.

Leorio bent down so our eyes were in line and the blue of mine reflected in his pupils. 'Earth will cut you down to size. Have no worries on that score.'

I wasn't sure what Leorio meant, but it was obvious he'd run out of patience. I was so confused, I couldn't think. 'How long will I be away?'

'That depends on you.' Leorio pressed a button on his intercom. 'Josef, take Omzak to the launch chamber. He's to leave for England immediately.' Leorio turned to me. 'Just to make things clear, the only reason I'm sending you on a leisure pod is because it's fast. That doesn't mean you're to take advantage of the services on-board.'

*This **is** happening*, I thought, my head spinning with questions. *Where in England am I going? How will I become a pet?*

'Did you hear me?' Leorio said.

'Yes, sir,' I said, saluting. I shuddered at the thought of what lay ahead.

2

This can't be Earth? Everything's ginormous

At any other time, a ride in a space pod might have been OK. The only vessels I'd been in were huge, bumpy warships, with tanks clattering on metal ramps. This was small and shaped like a rocket. And so quiet I could hear my breath.

Outside the portal, there wasn't much to see apart from squiggles of blue as night turned to day. I felt numb with shock for the first twenty-four hours but eventually settled down.

How bad could living amongst Earth cats be? So long as no one stroked me, I could be someone's *pet*. I'd heard all they did was sleep, anyway.

The thing driving me crazy was starvation. I hadn't eaten in two days. And there on the wall was a food-vending machine, loaded with packets of smoked kippers, caviar, barbequed prawns, grilled fillet steak...

But Leorio had forbidden me from using any of

the services on-board. I tucked my paws under my tail to resist temptation.

I was imagining chewing a tasty prawn when the pod shuddered to a halt. Below was a miserable looking town. It was shrouded in mist. The sky was overcast.

'You have arrived. This is your destination,' an automated voice said over chiming bells. The bottom of the pod opened. 'Unlock your safety belt.' As soon as I did, the floor under my chair fell away. 'Prepare to drop.'

I tumbled out, twisted upside down, went into a nose dive and ...

Splat!

I landed face down on a soggy mound that smelled of rotting cabbage. I picked myself up and spat out a bit of paper. I was shaking with horror. *I can't even empty a dustbin without coming out in a rash. Now I'm standing in one.* My scream echoed round the plastic walls. My heart was beating like a drum. *I'm having a heart attack!* I thought. I took a deep breath, leapt at the rim of the bin, gripped it and pulled myself up.

I looked down to see a mouse sitting on the ground below, eating a mouldy lump of cheese. It was the size of a monster rat. The bin was in an alley, and there were rows of sheds in it – they weren't normal size, either.

'Whoa!!' I said. 'This can't be Earth. Everything's ginormous.'

I jumped down. Strands of spaghetti plopped off my ears. 'Urrrrggggh – help!' I spotted a broken piece of mirror amongst a pile of rubbish and grabbed it. I looked at my reflection. My fur wasn't white any more. It was covered in blobs of red sauce. Hanging off my tail was loads more gooey spaghetti.

I shook my body to get it off. It was stuck like glue. Feeling sick, I picked off the bits. *I'm not shaking, I'm not having a heart attack, I haven't come out in a rash.*

As I picked off the last strand, the reason everything looked so huge hit me. I went into shock again. *It's because the dimensions on Earth are different. That's what Leorio meant when he said I'd be cut down to size.*

'I'm so small, everyone will think I'm a kitten.' I took a deep breath. 'See the funny side,' I told myself, going down on all fours.

I walked up and down to remember how to do it. It felt clumsy and stupid. Being so close to the ground was weird. And putrid smells were coming out of the drains. I held my breath so the stench didn't go up my nose. 'This punishment's even *worse* than kitchen duties!'

At the end of the alley was a busy street. There I was, a scrap of fur in a land of giants. There were lorries honking, music was blasting out of car

11

windows and pedestrians stomped along the pavement. I dodged a workman's boot, jumped clear of a pram about to crush my paws and weaved towards the traffic lights.

'What a cute kitten,' a girl said to her friend, bending down to stroke me.

I hissed like an Earth cat, thinking *'back off'* and marched across the zebra crossing. When I glanced up, I saw a sign – *Welcome to Mapulsbury*.

'Welcome to Mapulsbury,' I said under my breath. 'What a joke!' Compared to Catopia, it was a polluted dump. Catopia had two lilac suns hanging side by side, golden dunes stretching over the desert, and the air smelled of Popegus flowers. This was a tangle of ugly grey buildings under a grey sky, and it stank of exhaust fumes.

I kicked a paper cup off the curb. *How do I go about becoming a pet?* The answer was to ask an Earth cat, which meant I'd have to meow. Miserable, I turned into Mapulsbury high street.

A little way along, outside a place called George's Kebabs, was a cat. It had greasy, matted black fur, and was so huge it looked pregnant. It lay sprawled out in a wicker chair, snoring like a pig.

Close by, a man was sweeping dust away from the door. 'Hey, Zorba, when you gonna wake up and chase the mice from the kitchen?'

Zorba rolled on his belly and belched.

My nose twitched with disgust. If I'd found myself in the desert dying of thirst, I wouldn't have asked that scruffy, unkempt cat if he knew of a waterhole.

Further along, there was a shop selling medicines and remedies – a herbalist. I glanced up at a balcony above the shop window to see a female cat. This was a red Persian wearing a ruby-stone collar. She looked OK so I stopped, practised a couple of meows to get the hang of it and called out. 'Hey, you up there.'

The Persian, who was painting her claws, peered down. 'Ooh, does your mam know you're out? You're a bit small to be wandering the streets alone, chuck,' she purred.

I ignored the fact she called me *'chuck'*. Whatever it meant, it sounded like an insult. 'Could you tell me how I go about becoming a pet?' I meowed.

'Well, there's a funny question,' she replied, blowing on her claws.

'Oh, and the person should be someone who's looking for a short-term pet.'

'You've gorra funny accent and say your meows back to front. Take it yur not from round here?'

'I'm talking in the language of my ancestors – and I didn't expect to. Ever. And if anyone's got a funny accent, it's you,' I meowed.

'Picked it up from my minders. They're from

Manchester originally.' She tipped her nose in the air. 'Mind you, I always say it's breeding what counts.' She gave me a smile that made her face wrinkle like a prune. 'Name's Pasha, chuck.'

'As you can see, *Pasha*,' I pointed to my tail, which was banging the pavement, 'I'm not having a good day. Cut to the chase and stop wasting my time.' (Or I may have meowed, 'Chase the cut and stop my time wasting.')

Pasha poked her head through the railings. 'You've got froth on yur mouth.'

'Froth?' My paw flew to my lips. Then I realised what she meant. 'These are my whiskers. I've had them since I was two.'

'Oh, and how old are you now?' Pasha meowed.

'Fourteen.' I was getting more annoyed by the second.

'Really.' Pasha sniffed, as if she didn't believe me. 'Well, yur whiskers look like bicycle handlebars.'

'Do you know who you're talking to, Prune Face?' I stamped a forepaw, regretting it straight away. I kept forgetting she thought I was a kitten.

'You cheeky little monkey.' Pasha withdrew her head from the railings and started washing her face.

I looked about frantically. There wasn't another cat in sight.

'Just question my answer – I mean answer my question,' I meowed.

Pasha sniffed. 'What I think is, your mam threw you out because of bad behaviour.'

'I moved out because I felt like a change.'

'Well, I'm not encouraging you to be a runaway.' Pasha waved me away with her tail. 'Get back to your mam and say sorry.' She rose to all fours and sauntered off. 'And take those silly whiskers off.'

3

Jodie takes me in as her pet

In a street that led off Mapulsbury high street was a shop called Pet Paradise. The door was open and from where I stood it looked like pet hell. Kittens were caged as if awaiting execution. They were yowling like maniacs to make themselves heard over barking dogs, squeaky hamsters and a screechy monkey.

I was about to march off when a shadow fell over me. I looked up to see two boys wearing scuffed trainers and what looked like curtain rings in their ears.

'Look at that kitten's eyes. They're psychedelic blue', the first boy said.

'Its whiskers look like a colonel's moustache,' the second one added, laughing.

The first one pulled on his curtain ring. 'Must be a special breed.'

'D'ya think it's lost?' the other one asked.

'Dunno, let's take it in the pet shop.' His grimy hands swooped down to grab me.

I stood up on my hind legs and rolled my front paws into fists. 'Touch me with your filthy hands and I'll knock you flat,' I said.

'It's an alien!' the boy shrieked. 'We've been invaded by aliens.'

The boys took off like they had rockets under their feet. *From now on, keep your mouth shut,* I thought, getting back down on all fours.

I wandered through the backstreets. My stomach was groaning like a bear with toothache. I hated Earth, its cats and people. I wanted to go back home. *Home.* The word went round in my head. I missed my marble bathroom, my king-size bed, my grand piano, my ...

At 18 Uphill Park Road, I looked through the gate and saw a partly open window. I guessed it was the kitchen because a chocolaty smell was wafting out.

'This is more like it.' I crept across the garden, backflipped onto the window ledge and peered inside. No one was about. And sitting on the kitchen counter was a rack of steaming brownies.

Somersaulting over, I picked a bit up, blew on it and took a bite. In the middle it had crunchy toffee bits. It was so hot I had to whoosh it round my mouth.

'AATCHOOOO!' An explosion of a sneeze came from the hallway. The door opened.

I jumped to the floor.

A girl, about ten years old, came in. Her face was blotchy, her hair was sticking to her neck and she was trembling with fever. Shuddering at how many germs were swimming round her, I shuffled backwards.

'Hello, little kitty, what are you doing here?' She smiled. 'I'd stroke you but I'm sure you don't want my flu.' She blew in a hankie.

At least she won't touch me. That's something.

I knew from the reaction of the boys at the pet shop I couldn't answer, in case she handed me over to the police.

'Your eyes are bluer than the sea,' the girl said, bending down. 'What funny whiskers. You look like something from a comic book.' She looked at the plate of brownies. 'That's funny, there's a piece missing. You've got chocolate on your chin,' she said, giggling.

The girl went to a cupboard, took out a tin of cat food and pulled off the foil. 'This one's Horacio's favourite. He's my cat. It's chicken in gravy.'

She put it in a bowl, mashed it with a fork and set it down on the floor. The smell was disgusting. I couldn't imagine how Earth cats ate that junk.

'Go on, it's yummy.'

I backed away from the bowl and blinked. *You taste it if it's so yummy.*

The girl scratched a scab on her nose. 'Maybe later then.' She walked across to the sink and squeezed some liquid on a cloth. 'We'd better get you washed before my mum comes home. You've got sauce on your back.'

My whiskers shot up. I watched the cloth coming towards me and swerved clear.

'Don't you like being washed?'

I stared at her, thinking *'Not by you'*, then walked to the kitchen door.

'Where do you want to go?' the girl asked.

Guessing where the bathroom was, I marched up the stairs and sat outside it.

'You're so cute. Are you trying to tell me you want to wash yourself?' she said.

I nodded. It seemed a safe bet.

The girl turned the shower on and watched me expectantly. I kept looking towards the door until she took the hint.

As soon as she was gone, I jumped under the shower and scrubbed myself from head to tail Then I somersaulted over to the sink and quickly combed my coat.

I'd just finished when the doorknob clicked. I backflipped to the ground and sat there, a picture of innocence.

The girl walked round me in a circle. 'How did you get yourself so clean? How did …'

I gave nothing away, listening to a key turn in a lock downstairs.

'Quick, that's my mum,' the girl said. 'I'll hide you in my bedroom. And don't start meowing because she won't let me keep you.'

Whoa. I don't even have to meow in this house.

I followed her into the bedroom. She put a finger to her lips and closed the door.

I looked around her room. Standing against one wall was a piano. On another there was a bookcase crammed with history books. I was better at history than anyone on my planet. *We could test each other on our knowledge if I didn't have to pretend I'm an Earth cat.*

A frenzied scream filled the house. Footsteps thudded up the stairs.

I hid behind a curtain.

The girl came in and slammed the door. 'I'm *not* going back to school. I hate it, hate it.' She threw herself on the bed and thumped it with her fists.

A woman, her cheeks puffed out like plums, ran in and went to the girl's bed. 'Don't you dare walk away when I'm talking to you, Jodie,' she said, shaking one of the girl's legs. 'As soon as you're well you *are* going back to school. I'm your mother and you'll do as I say.'

Jodie kicked her leg free and sat up. 'Chloe Jackson is the troublemaker, not me!' she said, narrowing her eyes like an angry witch.

'You kicked her in the knee,' her mother said, dragging her hands through her hair.

'Because she's pathetic,' Jodie shouted.

'This is the second time you've been suspended.' Her mother wagged a finger. 'One more time and you'll be expelled.'

'Good. I want to be expelled. No one gets me at that school.'

'Because you think you're too good for everyone,' her mother said.

The girl buried her head in a pillow. 'Leave me alone.'

Jodie's mother threw her hands in the air. 'I've had just about enough,' she said, banging the door as she left.

I couldn't believe my ears. *Jodie is a replica of me.*

That night I was given a hiding place under Jodie's bed. The carpet had itchy bobbles, and even worse was having her above me. Every time she moved the bed bumped, the mattress croaked and the springs twanged. When she wasn't sneezing, she coughed up what reminded me of gloopy frog spawn.

If I'm going to be holed up here, I need to do something about her flu, I thought. I got up, quiet as a mouse, and crept out of the open bedroom window without a sound.

4

I swear I'm not a deluded kitten

I arrived outside the herbalist shop and began looking for signs of Pasha. There were steps leading down to a basement. At the bottom was a door with a cat flap. It was painted lilac and had a knocker shaped like a bunch of roses. *That's definitely her place,* I thought.

I padded down the stairs on all fours but at the bottom I pulled myself up to standing. *If Pasha is going to help she needs to know I'm a famous space cat warrior.* I lifted the knocker and rapped. *She should count herself lucky I am even gracing her doorstep.*

The cat flap opened. Pasha yawned. 'Don't tell me your mam threw you out again.' She licked a paw and wiped the sleep from her eyes.

I gave her my best smile and pushed past. 'We need to talk.'

'Still no *please* – kittens of today,' Pasha meowed. 'You'll get crooked legs if yur not careful. I was three before my minders sent me to learn how to stand.'

What, she can stand? I thought, momentarily taken aback. I made a note to ask Pasha the details when I had less to worry about.

'So what do you want to talk about? Pasha meowed catching up with me.

'A lot of stuff,' I said.

'Well, it had better be good. You're getting five minutes and that's yur lot.'

Pasha sauntered off to get a rubber mat. This was in case I had any 'little accidents', as she said. I bit my tongue so that I didn't say anything rude.

While she was gone I had a good look round her den. There was a bicycle leaning against the wall, but from the look of it, it hadn't been used in years. The rug was littered with peach frilly cushions, and on the wall was a portrait of Pasha wearing a tiara. Next to that was a certificate giving details of her heritage. I stretched my neck to see the title of the book sitting on the table. *How to Marry Into Royalty – who does Prune Face think she is?* was my first thought. My second was since *when* had Earth cats learned to read?

Pasha came back through a curtain that divided the room.

'Sit,' she meowed through a mouthful of rubber, before dropping the mat in front of me.

'I don't know where it's been,' I meowed. 'You can't really expect me to sit on that?'

24

'Sit – or leave.'

I perched without letting my lower body touch the mat, watching Pasha flick out the frill on her cushion. 'Go on. I'm listening.'

I looked away from the pom-pom jumper she'd put on, so I could concentrate.

I spoke slowly to get my meows right. I began with my meeting in Leorio's chambers, bending the truth a bit. Pasha listened without moving until I finished.

'So yur telling me you landed in a dustbin but you're not a stray, because in Catopia you're a famous warrior who's the equivalent of a four-foot cat?' she meowed, her tail swishing to and fro. 'Have I got that right?' Pasha turned her ears to face me.

'Yes,' I meowed.

'And because of your kindness and compassion, yur ruler sent you here to befriend a child?' she meowed.

'Yeah.'

'And now you've come here to fetch medicine because that child is sick?'

'Exactly.'

Pasha's paw flew out and clipped me round the ear. My mouth dropped open in disbelief. 'You'll get another one if you don't stop telling fibs.' She neatly crossed her forepaws, as if reminding herself she had a pedigree.

I drew myself up on my hind legs. 'If you do that again, you'll be the one getting a paw round your ear,' I meowed.

Pasha's eyes darted about as if she was following an invasion of flies. 'I know – have you had a knock on your head?'

'No!' I moved off the mat. The rubbery smell was making me feel sick.

Pasha fanned herself with her tail. 'In which case, you could be suffering with delusion. I was reading an article about it the other day.'

'Delusion?' I screwed up my face. 'I've got no idea what you're on about.'

'There was a kitten who thought he was a bird and broke his paws trying to fly. And another who thought she was a dog and...'

'I'm not suffering with delusion. I'm a Catopian who, amongst loads of other stuff, has a grade A diploma in herbal medicine. If I break one jar, if I throw herbs about, you can turf me out. You could help a child who's *really* sick,' I added, looking at the ceiling for inspiration. 'Please let me into the shop.'

Pasha looked at me like a teacher appraising a pupil. 'I suppose, since you've said please,' she purred, examining her manicured claws. 'And since you're such a hoity-toity herbalist, what remedy might you make for me?'

26

'A brilliant potion to give you fur like a princess,'
I meowed, remembering the title of her book.

Pasha lifted a hind leg out to the side and ran a
paw down its pampered length. 'And when might
you do that?'

'I'll come back whenever you like,' I meowed.

Pasha pursed her lips. 'Can't believe I'm being
persuaded by a kitten.'

She stared at my whiskers. 'On the other hand,
you're not like any I've ever met.'

'Because I'm not a kitten,' I meowed. 'Now can
we,' I pointed to the door that led to the herbalist
shop, 'get on with it?'

There was a *ratatatat* on the cat flap.

Pasha's green eyes flashed like light bulbs. 'I'll
just deal with this first.' She marched to the flap and
opened it. 'I told you to sling yur hook,' she hissed.

'I've come to tell you I love you,' a tomcat outside
meowed.

'Well, you can shove off. I want more from life
than a lazy lump of lard with no prospects.' Pasha
slammed the flap shut. 'Sorry 'bout that, chuck,' she
meowed to me. 'That Zorba gets on my blimmin'
nerves!'

Zorba? Where had I heard that name before? If it
was the same scruff ball I'd come across, I didn't
blame her for wanting nothing to do with him.

'Come on then,' Pasha meowed, gesturing for me

to follow her. Her face took on a pinched look, as if she was imagining jars smashing to the ground. 'My minders will never let me hear the end of it if you destroy the shop.'

Pasha led me into the shop and jumped up on the counter. I could feel her eyes boring into my neck. I pretended she wasn't there and ran my eyes along the shelves. There were six in all, stretching along the back wall. Each one was packed with containers of every size. I read the labels, making mental notes. 'Got a small cardboard box and some small plastic bags?' I meowed.

'Cardboard box under the counter, plastic bags in the top drawer,' Pasha indicated.

I found the bags, put them in the box and wedged it between two steps of the sliding ladder. 'If you're nervous, look away,' I meowed, ready to give her the show of her life. I grabbed a plastic bag, clambered up the ladder to the top shelf, then took hold of a jar of nettle leaves. In Catopia, where everything was smaller, I'd have been able to grasp the jar with one paw and use the other to open it. *How was I going to prise the top off?*

'You'd better not drop that,' Pasha meowed.

I threw the jar in the air to shock her. Pasha covered her eyes and screamed. 'I should never have let you …' She peeked at me over a paw.

'What's your problem,' I meowed, catching the jar

and shaking it like a cocktail. Clamping my teeth round the top of the jar, I yanked it off. I tipped some of the leaves into the plastic bag, closed the jar and put it back.

Pasha's expression changed from 'ready to have a hissing fit' to one of awe. 'Ooh, you didn't spill a single leaf,' she meowed.

I wiggled my whiskers. 'Watch this.'

Using a hind paw I pushed the sliding ladder along the wall and started collecting herbs from various jars at such dizzying speed that Pasha's eyes were soon spinning. I dropped the bags of herbs one by one into the box.

'How many more do you need?' She sounded flustered. 'I think I can hear one of my minders walking about.'

'One more. I left this for last.' I tipped myself upside down, wound my tail around a rung of the ladder and eased a heavier jar off the shelf using all four paws. I pulled the top off, sprinkled some of the contents in a plastic bag, replaced the jar and flipped back onto the counter with a double back somersault.

'Eee, that was good.' Pasha clapped her paws.

I reached for an empty pot and started filling it with a variety of herbs. 'Got something to carry this in?' I meowed.

'You'll find a pouch second drawer to the left.'

I found one and nodded. 'We'll hide the box of herbs in your den,' I meowed, tucking the pot in the pouch.

Pasha pinned back her ears, listening intently. 'Quick, back to me den – one of me minders is coming!'

5

Jodie throws me out

When I climbed back in through Jodie's window she was lying in bed with a flannel over her eyes. She wasn't asleep. I could see her fingers tapping the duvet as if she was playing a tune in her head.

On her bedside table was a bottle of medicine. Silently, I leapt onto the table, picked up the bottle, took it to the window and emptied it. I filled it with my own remedy, which I had quickly prepared back in Pasha's den, and was creeping back when Jodie sat up.

And there I was, standing upright, with the evidence in my paws.

Jodie fanned her face with the flannel. 'I must be dreaming.'

'I've brought you a remedy to cure you before I die of contamination,' I blurted out.

'Did you just say something?' Jodie said.

'I've been sent from Catopia to … to be your

friend. Name's Omzak,' I said, walking towards her.

Jodie giggled. 'This dream's cool.'

'Look, I forgot myself. I didn't mean to talk. But I am real, honest.'

Jodie nodded in a trance and wiped her forehead. 'I must be hallucinating, or something.'

'Let me prove you're not hallucinating,' I said, jumping on her bedside table. 'I made this for you and it will heal you a hundred times faster than what you were taking.' I held out my remedy. 'If you take ten sips on the hour, your flu will be gone before you know it.'

'You're not real. Kittens can't talk.' Jodie reached out to stroke my tail.

I jumped back. 'If you don't believe me, I can tell you every word that passed between you and your mother last night,' I said.

'Like what?' Jodie said, tugging at her lanky hair.

'You were suspended from school for kicking Chloe Jackson in the knee.'

Jodie blew out a stream of breath. 'Because I like history more than playing stupid games, that's why!' She squinted at me. 'I'm ending this dream right now. Go away, freak.'

She blinked rapidly. Her face was so red it looked ready to crack. I was overcome with panic. If Jodie's mother came back and saw me, I'd never get back in the house. That meant I'd have to start from the beginning and find someone else to take me in as a pet.

'So, you're good at history. Bet I'm better than you,' I said.

Jodie screwed up her lips. 'I'm the best at everything.'

'All right, let's see. Shall I ask you anything I want?'

Jodie shrugged her shoulders. 'Make it hard.'

I gave my whiskers a twirl. 'Which king took the throne in England in 1714?'

'George the first – who spoke no English.' Jodie tut-tutted, as if the question was too easy. She looked at the ceiling, warming to the game. 'Ask me something else.'

'Who got shot through the eye at the Battle of Hastings in 1066?' I said.

'You didn't need to say the year.' Jodie tutted again. 'Harold the second was shot through the eye.'

'Not bad.'

Jodie gave a toss of her head. 'I knew *that* when I was five.'

'OK then, bet you don't know the answer to this.'

'Duhhhhh,' Jodie drawled, sneezing out more germs. 'I never get questions wrong.' She blew her fringe from her eyes.

'Who inhabited the world first, humans or Catopians?'

Jodie rolled her eyes then drew out the word humans so that it sounded like hummmmmm-aaaaaans.

'Wrong. Catopians are descendents of the Miacis, weasel-like creatures that lived on Earth forty million years ago.'

'Well, I've never heard of the *Miacis*,' Jodie said, wiping her nose on the sleeve of her pyjamas. 'I'm going to look it up.'

'While you're looking, you can look up Bast, one of my great, great relatives. He was revered as a cat god in ancient Egypt.'

'That's not history, that's stupid.' Her eyes had a malicious glint. 'So why don't Catopians live on Earth now then?'

'Because we evolved and moved to our own planet.'

Jodie snapped out of her dreamlike trance. She shook her head until her hair was flapping across her forehead.

'That's ... that's ... I'm not listening. Go away. Shoo!'

A strand of her hair hit me in the eye. I jumped to the floor to get out of the way. 'If you're real, you're a bad kitten. *And* a big liar.' Jodie stopped shaking her head to listen to herself. She was breathing hard. 'I'm talking to a kitten.' Her body went floppy, as if she couldn't make sense of what had gone on.

I pricked up my ears. I could hear the crunch of shopping trolley wheels on the gravel.

Jodie narrowed her eyes at me. 'I'm not taking any of your stupid medicine. You're trying to poison me. Go away or I'll … I'll call the … the RSPCA.' She gave the medicine bottle a slap and knocked it on the carpet.

I jumped clear as the bottle smashed to pieces, sending a stream of liquid trickling everywhere.

Footsteps.

I could hear the tap of heels coming up the stairs.

'If Leorio thinks I'm arrogant, he should try spending a day with you!' I jumped onto the windowsill, wanting to throttle her. 'I probably won't come back,' I said.

6

How bad can this get?

I don't know what's worse; having to deal with a bratty child or finding myself back here with Prune Face.

I rapped Pasha's knocker. When she didn't answer, I thumped hard until she did.

'*Meeeooow!*' Pasha squealed, narrowly missing a fist in her eye.

'It's me who should be squealing in fright,' I meowed. 'Do you have any idea what you look like?' Pasha pointed to her face. It was covered in thick paste. 'I dunked it in a bowl of yoghurt. It's a beauty treatment,' she mumbled.

'Well, could you clean it off? I need some advice,' I meowed, pushing her aside.

Squinting, Pasha disappeared to wash her face. I threw myself down on a cushion and lay there feeling sorry for myself.

'You came back quickly,' Pasha meowed.

'It went a bit wrong.'

'Why was that, chuck?'

'Because Jodie's a child from hell. D'you know what she did? She knocked that remedy I made her on the floor.'

'Ooh, and after all that hard work,' Pasha purred.

I leapt to my feet. 'You'd have thought a girl who's got a Catopian for a pet could have shown a bit of appreciation.' I tapped my chest fiercely. 'I have four medals on my military jacket.'

'D'you think you're wearing a military jacket now, chuck?' Pasha meowed.

I knew she thought I was crazy. 'I'm talking about my jacket in Catopia.'

'What were your ruler's orders, exactly?' Pasha asked, washing her ears.

'My orders were to be an ambassador of … intergalactic harmony,' I replied.

'Then yur ruler should have sent someone else because you get on everyone's nerves.'

'Are you going to help me or not?' I meowed.

She stood on all fours, gave her back legs a stretch then sauntered to my side. 'Maybe this will help, we call this a friendship rub,' she meowed. 'All you have to do is rub your head against Jodie's ankles.'

Pasha showed me what she meant, purring all the while, then looked up at me like she was sucking a bag of sugar.

'Get off. I'm not doing that.'

'Well, since you can't bring yourself to try my suggestion, you'll have to say sorry for frightening Jodie to death.'

'*Frightening her*? I was so amazing, I amazed myself with how amazing I was,' I meowed, my eyes darting round the room. 'Where did you put the box? I'll start by making her another bottle of medicine – a sort of token to say sorry.'

'I can't risk me minders coming in and catching you at it chuck, so it'll have to wait 'til early tomorrow morning.' Pasha narrowed her eyes – 'when I shall also be expecting the potion yur making *me*.' She waited until I nodded.

'And since you can't stay here, and you can't stay at Jodie's for now, I've arranged with a friend for you to stay with him,' she added.

'I'm not living with an Earth cat!'

'Oh, I thought you came to promote intergalactic relationships?'

'Living amongst Earth cats and staying with one are two entirely different matters,' I objected.

'Yur other option is to sleep rough in the woods, but you'll have vampire mosquitoes sucking at your blood.'

'Eww! I suppose I could manage *one* night with your friend.'

Pasha had temporarily forgotten me and was nibbling between her claws.

'You said "he", so I'm guessing he's a male?' I meowed.

Pasha stopped nibbling. 'Ooh, aye, a very macho tom.'

'Does he have somewhere to wash?' I asked.

'Big tap in his yard.' Pasha smoothed her ruff over her ruby collar, then stood on all fours and gave her body a shake. 'And he lives close enough for me to keep my eye on you.'

7

All Earth cats are nuts

The walk to Pasha's friend's house nearly made me die of embarrassment. Spending time in her den had been a challenge – but being seen with her in public was fifty times worse. I was a third of her size and felt like a kitten out for a stroll with its mother. The good thing was I could walk much faster than her.

Behind me, I could hear Pasha meowing at me to slow down but I took no notice until I reached the corner. There I stopped, because I didn't know which way to go.

I watched Pasha trot towards me, tongue lolling out and panting. Unable to speak, she pointed an ear at a yard next door to George's Kebabs.

My eyes narrowed. Surely Pasha couldn't be bringing me to stay with the tomcat that only yesterday she'd called 'a lump of lard'?

Pasha nudged me with her nose. 'Go on, get in,' she meowed.

I went in to see Zorba lumbering towards me like a bear.

I glared at Pasha. She was pretending to pick fluff off her blouse.

I stood up on two legs and gave Zorba a cold stare. If I was to be this lump of lard's guest, I needed to lay down the rules.

I was caught unawares when Zorba's hefty paw slapped me on the shoulder. 'Welcome, my new littlee friend,' he meowed, nodding in admiration. A soft whistling sound came out of his mouth. 'I see you can walk on two legs, the same way as Pasha. And may I say what *fine* whiskers you have.'

Zorba gave a hearty burp then, like a conspirator, brought his mouth to my ear. 'Pasha tells me you are crazy, but I like that you are different. So, whatever you need, whatever you like, you tell Zorba, eh?'

I flapped away Zorba's stinky garlic breath. As I did, Zorba pinched my cheek.

'We are going to have a good time together,' he meowed.

My paw flew up to bop Zorba on the nose.

Before it made contact, Pasha jumped between us. 'Zorba's very good at making things. Show Omzak your new invention, chuck.' She pushed Zorba out of the way, headbutting his backside. He sighed as if he'd been touched by an angel and lumbered off across the yard.

'So, you think I'm *crazy*!' I meowed to Pasha. I sat on my haunches, folded my forepaws over my chest and pressed down hard to trap them there. The thought of all the germs in that yard was really making me itch. 'I've never seen such a scruffy cat. I'm struggling not to scratch myself raw.'

'I know Zorba's a bit smelly and doesn't have table manners but he's got his good points,' Pasha said. 'When you know him, you'll get on like peas in a pod.'

'I hate peas.' I looked around the yard. 'Bringing me to this pigsty. Somebody should put that hosepipe away. And what's the point of a three-legged table, a rickety chair and a hammock with holes?'

'I think it's homely,' Pasha meowed.

Yeah, right, I thought. She wouldn't have lasted five minutes in this dump.

I watched a fly settle on Zorba's food bowl and feed on the grease on its rim. 'Urgh.' I started to itch again.

A piece of metal clattered to the floor inside the coal bunker that stood inside the yard. I turned to look. A hole that had been sawn out of the bottom and served as a door was filling with Zorba's rear. His black tail wagging like a flag, he jiggled his backside free. His stomach got stuck. He couldn't budge. I wanted to grab him and fling him over the wall.

42

'Get yur flamin' belly out,' Pasha urged, sensing I was losing my patience.

A moment later, Zorba's head came out. Tugging a piece of string, he pulled out a wooden platform that had some sort of contraption sitting on top. 'This is my mouse catcher,' he meowed, tapping a tube that stuck out from a box.

He gave Pasha a wink, wiped his greasy paws and pawed out a piece of cheese. 'I put this cheese on a wire inside the box and when the mouse goes for it, a ball falls down the tube and hits its head.' Zorba opened his forepaws like he was inviting the world in for a hug. 'I can show you how it works.'

'No thanks,' I meowed.

Zorba scratched his belly. 'Maybe you'd like to see my clock that meows the time?'

'You're nuts,' I replied. 'I'm going for a walk.'

8

Tell you what – let's cut a deal

After I'd cooled down I went back to Zorba's. He was stretched out, his head drooping over his paws. He raised one eye then went on staring at the floor. 'If only someone could explain *why* Pasha doesn't love me.' Zorba gave such a wide yawn I saw down his throat. 'If I could, I would give her every star in the sky. I would buy her a collar with emeralds.' He pushed his heavy bulk into a sitting position.

'Who knows?' I meowed, looking away from the greasy globs on his chest.

Zorba looked in my eyes. 'I have the honour of having in my house a famous warrior from Planet Catopia – who came to Earth to befriend a child.'

I squirmed with discomfort. He didn't know the real story.

'Tell me what I am doing wrong,' Zorba meowed.

'I don't know. The girls I like won't go out with me either.'

'Why? What they say?' Zorba asked.

I wasn't going to tell him they said I was too big for my boots. 'That I'm too dedicated to being a warrior,' I said.

Zorba sighed, blasting me with the smell of garlic.

'Yuck, your breath stinks,' I complained. 'Move back a bit.'

Zorba shuffled backwards. 'Tell me. You must know something.'

The smell of garlic had worked its way into my whiskers. I rubbed at them, feeling sick. 'OK, I'll tell you – but you're not going to like it.'

Zorba punched himself in the chest. 'I'm a tomcat through to my feet. Say your worst.'

'Your fur's filthy, you're fat, sloppy and you've got bad body odour.'

Zorba sniffed his armpits then hugged his belly. 'What, you are saying I am smelly? Why has no one told me this before?' He set to work licking the grease off his chest and gestured to his bowl of leftovers. 'I'm going to change myself straight after we have some food.' Zorba smacked his lips. 'Plenty for us both.'

'You've got enough food in your belly to last a year. If you're serious about Pasha, you need to get rid of that pouch.' I rubbed my ruff, which itched like a town of fleas. 'And licking yourself isn't going to get that muck off. This isn't the dark ages. You need to stand under the tap and scrub it off.'

'OK. So you give me a diet, some exercises to get slimmer and stand up like ...'

'I haven't got time for that. I'm here on Earth for specific reasons,' I meowed. As I said 'specific reasons', an idea came to me. 'Tell you what, let's cut a deal.'

'Anything,' Zorba meowed, swatting a fly and missing.

'I'm making Jodie another remedy to cure her flu, but I know something that works much faster,' I explained, thinking about how impressed Leorio would be with my efforts. 'Everyone round here calls you the inventor, right?'

'It's true,' Zorba agreed.

'If I give you the design for a wrist-worn healing device, could you put one together?'

'I was hearing about something like this. We put magnets in a bracelet, turn it on like a clock and it sends energy around the body to make it strong,' said Zorba.

I was impressed, in spite of myself. 'Yeah. A magnetosphere.'

'Deal,' said Zorba.

'But your first job is to have a scrub,' I instructed, somersaulting onto the washing line and taking down a clean towel.

'That's kind of you,' Zorba meowed, thinking I was getting it for him.

'This is for me to sleep on,' I said, carrying it to the coal bunker. I looked inside at the pile of junk. 'And tomorrow you'd better clean this up because I'm *not* sleeping in a pigsty.'

9

The ballet-dancing tomcat

The next morning, when I got to Pasha's, she was painting another cat's claws. She'd placed a tea towel over a cushion to protect it and was elegantly draped over one side. Jiggling like jelly on the other side was a pink-furred Siamese called Floss. His meows were so high, it sounded like he had a pin stuck up his nose.

'And then these vicious cats attacked me.' Floss shrilled, retelling a story about a gang of cats who'd set on him in an alley. 'Boof, boof, boof,' he screeched, mimicking the sound of when one of them had socked him in the eye.

Pasha let out a hysterical meow, as if the fight was happening for real.

The herbs in my paws scattered over the piece of wood I'd set up as a workbench. 'Could you try not to get so excited,' I meowed, gathering them back up and emptying them into a jar.

'Floss flapped a paw at me. 'Sorry Captain Omzak.'

'So you should be,' I meowed. 'And stop talking to me so I can concentrate.'

'Fine lovey,' Floss said. 'I'll tell Pasha what I'm going to say in the goodbye note I'll leave when you take me back with you.'

I'd already told Floss that Earth cats couldn't relocate to Catopia so I didn't bother to comment.

'I'll start it by saying,' Floss meowed to Pasha. 'To those who loved me, and the horrid brutes who couldn't see past their whiskers to appreciate my sensitive qualities.'

Pasha nodded. 'Very poetic chuck.'

I switched off. Floss's note was the length of a novel.

When he'd finished, he twirled his slender neck to

49

check my progress with Pasha's potion. 'When your mix is ready, can I use a bit Pasha?'

'Course you can, chuck,' Pasha meowed.

'Ommmmmmmzakkkkk,' Floss shrilled, making my teeth go funny. 'Will it make my fur thick and lush? I'd quite like having long hair for a change.'

Floss's fur was so short and see-through he looked like a newly shorn sheep. 'This mixture's not magic,' I meowed. Distracted by Floss's interruption, I mistakenly added an extra spoonful of one of the ingredients.

Pasha patted Floss's paw. His nose was quivering. 'Take no notice, chuck,' Pasha meowed.

Floss blinked away a tear, flapped a paw and purred. 'At least you're honest, lovey.'

'Floss's hobbies are boxing – which he's a real champ at – and ballet dancing. He's got a lovely tutu,' Pasha said.

'It's divine. My minders brought it back from Paris. It's fluorescent pink with little pearls,' Floss explained.

I shook Pasha's mixture and held up the bottle. 'I've kept my promise. See you around.'

'Even if I can't come to Catopia,' Floss gushed, 'while you're here I want us to be the best, best, best of friends.' He sniffled and flapped a paw. 'It means more to me than meows can say that you love me for who I am.'

Yeah, right, I thought, wondering what had made him think that, when I couldn't stand the sight of him.

10

Getting back in Jodie's good books

Jodie's front garden wasn't big, but there was lots of foliage to hide behind. I chose a hollow between two bushes and settled down to wait.

I lowered my body on my forepaws. Being close to the ground meant I could study nature in microscopic detail – like the team of ants that were hauling the carcass of a beetle over a stone. I knew ants could carry up to fifty times their weight but watching them this close was riveting. Every so often, the ant at the front stopped to raise a leg.

'Forward! Pull! Over the hill to victory,' I said, imagining him giving orders. I sat up and looked about guiltily, in case anyone had been listening.

Someone had come out of the house and shut the front door.

I poked my nose through the bush to see Jodie's mother walk to the gate. A few seconds later Jodie came out and started walking in my direction.

'Omzak, if you're here, please come out,' she called.

I smoothed my fur and stood up. 'I was just checking – for greenfly,' I said, mentally kicking myself for coming out with something so pathetic.

Jodie grinned. 'You look like a walking teddy bear. A-tchoo, aaaat-chooo!' She showered me with germs.

I covered my face. 'Either sneeze on yourself, or use a hankie.' I took a pawful of leaves and wiped myself.

'Sorry, it happened before I could use it,' she said, waving one. 'Do you want me to wipe your face? It's clean.'

'No, I'm fine – but the thought of germs makes my whiskers twitch.'

'I feel like that when someone gives me porridge.' Jodie made a face to show how much she hated it.

I couldn't see how germs and porridge were the same, but since I was her temporary pet, I played along. 'Yuck, porridge, totally disgusting.'

Jodie pulled her woolly shawl tighter round her neck, then bent down to stroke me.

'If I'm going to be your pet, another rule is I don't like being touched,' I said, stepping back.

Jodie hid her hands. 'OK. That's two things I have to remember. Can we sit on the grass for five minutes?'

I shrugged, brought my tail round to one side and settled on my haunches.

'Another reason I want to sit here is in case Horacio comes back,' Jodie said. 'He's been gone for two days.' She ran her fingers through the grass.

'He's bound to come back,' I said.

Nodding, Jodie turned away and sneezed into her shawl. 'I couldn't find out anything about Catopia, but I checked what you said about the Miacis and your ancestor, Bast. Now I believe you,' she said. 'And I'm sorry I broke the medicine bottle.'

I patted my whiskers. At least she accepted she'd behaved like a brat!

Jodie rubbed her crusty nose. Her eyes looked puzzled. 'You know the medicine you made me – did you bring it from Catopia?' Jodie asked.

'I made it in a herbalist shop on Mapulsbury High Street,' I said. 'There's a new pot of it hidden in that bush.' I stood up and gave my legs a shake.

'I don't understand,' Jodie said. 'What did you say to the people who owned the shop?'

'Nothing. Never met them,' I said.

Jodie screwed her nose up. 'So how did you get in?'

I told her about Prune Face and how I'd persuaded her to let me make a remedy. Jodie's eyes rounded like an owl's.

'What, you can talk to me and you know cat

language as well?' She clapped her hands in excitement. 'Tell me more about Pasha.'

I pointed to the house. 'Only if we go in. You're shivering.'

Once we were in the kitchen, Jodie tipped a tin of sardines on a plate. They tasted oily but it was better than eating at Zorba's, where the food crawled with flies.

'I've never seen a kitten stand on a chair and eat with a fork before,' Jodie said. 'When Horacio comes home he won't mind you living here.' She pointed to a picture of her cuddling a cat. It had a brown face with white patches. 'That's him.'

'Would you say he's a good pet?' I asked.

'He's the best. Loves being tickled on his tummy, but he's very independent.'

'So, to be a pet, I don't have to live here full time?' I said.

'No.' Jodie sneezed into her sleeve.

'I'll stay at Zorba's till your flu's gone.'

'Zorba?'

'He lives in a yard behind a kebab shop. We're working on a magnetosphere for you to wear on your wrist.'

'What does that do?' Jodie turned her head away to have another sneeze.

'It strengthens your immune system when you

come down with something like you've got now,' I said. 'A magnetosphere can cure you in half an hour.'

'Wow!' she said. 'Zorba's helping you make me a magnetothingamy. That's *so* cool.' Jodie pulled her chair closer to the table. 'Tell me about him,' she said, rattling off a hundred questions.

I told her what Zorba looked like, that I'd put him on a diet and what a klutz he was for being in love with Prune Face.

'Where's Zorba now?' Jodie said.

'I left him running round his yard chanting a mantra.' I gave the biggest burp. The sardines had upset me. I walked down the kitchen counter to stop any wind coming out.

'A *mantra*, what's that?' Jodie asked, watching me clutch my stomach.

'Something you keep repeating until you reach a goal you've set yourself.'

'Can I have a mantra?' Jodie said, picking at some threads on her jeans.

'What's your goal? Blluuuuuu ...' A bit of wind came out. I coughed to cover it up.

'To have a best friend and –' Jodie tapped her lips '– to give my best ever performance when I play at the Pavilion.'

'OK.' I twirled my whiskers. 'Your mantra is: I deserve to have a best friend because I'm worth it.

And I'm the most dazzling piano player in the universe.'

'I'm going to say it every day,' Jodie said, bringing her palm up to face me. 'Let's high five.'

'High five?' I said.

'It means we're friends, but we can do it to mean anything we want. Put your paw up and slap my hand.'

I raised a forepaw and tapped her palm.

'Now say high five,' Jodie said.

'High five. *Bluuuuuu* ... Better get back and see how Zorba's getting on,' I said, walking backwards.

11

Cats start to go missing

When I got back to Zorba's yard, I could hear glasses clinking and people singing. The sounds were coming from the kebab shop next door, where Zorba's minder was roasting chickens. With that temptation under his nose, I'd expected to see Zorba

stuffing his face. Instead, he was working on the magnetosphere and chanting his mantra.

'It is not my fault I am fat,' Zorba meowed. 'My minder gives me too much food, but it is my choice if I eat or not. And I say "yes" to good health.'

I was about to say 'hi' when Zorba gave his backside a waggle and started meowing again. 'And I choose to be the most handsome tomcat in Mapulsbury – Persians with green eyes will fall in love with me. And I choose to …'

I couldn't help grinning. 'What? You don't like my new verse?' Zorba looked hurt.

'If it works for you,' I meowed.

Zorba patted his belly, which echoed like a deflating plastic ball. 'You said only water until tomorrow, then I can have one kebab or one small piece of chicken.'

I nodded, doubting he'd last that long.

Zorba bit at his neck as if he was chasing a flea and cocked an ear at my diagram of the magnetosphere. 'I made a few changes to the design. All I need are two more pieces. My friend at the ironmonger's said he will get them tomorrow.'

'Good.' I pointed to the coal bunker. 'Did you clean it up?'

Zorba nodded. 'And I changed the cover in the basket because you have your scratchy disease.'

'Think I'll go get washed up then,' I said.

At that moment, three ginger tabby cats bounded into the yard. Skidding to a halt, they stood up on their hind legs and, puffing like trains, pointed to their mouths.

'Give us a moment,' they meowed together.

They were bouncing about as if they had springs under their paws. Every time they hit the concrete, their claws tapped out the exact same rhythm.

'Hold on,' they meowed, fanning each other's mouths.

All three had mustard-coloured eyes. And five stripes running down their fronts.

'The only way to tell who is who is to look at their tails,' Zorba meowed, picking up on my thoughts. 'Onesy has one stripe.'

Onesy, still panting, curtsied and pointed to it.

'Twosy has two stripes.'

Twosy did the same.

'And Threesy has three stripes.'

Threesy hurriedly pointed them out.

'We've just run all the way from Maccles,' the triplets meowed. 'And somethin's not right.' They wiped the sweat off their faces. 'Loads of cats have gone missing.'

Zorba went rigid. 'Did you speak to Ponch?'

'He's gone missing,' the triplets meowed.

I didn't know which cat to look at. When they

spoke, their mouths opened and closed together. When they moved, every gesture was identical.

Zorba turned to me to tell me the story. Not that I really cared.

'A few years ago, we had a big problem. The story was in the local newspaper. Men came with vans and stole hundreds of us.'

Curiosity got the better of me. 'Why would they do that?' I asked.

'Maybe to make us into chow mein and curries,' Zorba meowed.

I raised an eyebrow. 'What?'

'Some restaurants cook cats,' Zorba explained.

It was the most ridiculous theory I'd ever heard. I shrugged my shoulders and waited for the triplets to leave so I could get on with having a wash.

'What we gonna do, Zorb?' meowed the triplets.

'I will send a message to Tickles, the uncle of my fourth cousin. He knows everything in Maccles,' Zorba reassured them.

Tickles. I shook my head. The names minders gave their cats were pathetic.

'Tickles is one of the cats what's gone missing,' the triplets meowed hysterically.

Zorba's brown eyes brimmed with tears. He rolled his paw into a fist and thumped his heart. 'Later I'll go to Maccles, to find these people who kidnapped my uncle.'

It was like watching a tragic play, but audience or not, I preferred the shower option. 'I'm going to have a wash.'

The triplets gave me a curious sniff and looked at me like they'd just noticed me. 'So, who ya babysittin' then?' they meowed.

'Listen, you freaks, if you don't want trouble you'd …'

'This is Omzak – from Planet Catopia.'

Zorba patted my head before I saw it coming. I pushed his cheeks out of shape. 'Try that again and you're getting it.'

'He's a famous four-foot warrior,' Zorba meowed, with me still squishing his face.

I brushed my fur down. 'Just remember that.'

'Sure,' Zorba said, not in the least bit bothered. 'Omzak's a specialist in martial arts, warfare and many things – and he speaks English like a human.'

The triplets poked each other's bellies, meowing with laughter. 'What you been drinkin', Zorb?'

'Do not make fun of my little littlee friend.' He gave me a wink of friendship. 'We are making a magnetosphere bracelet together.'

'It's a healing device,' I clarified.

The triplets gathered round me like I was a freak of nature.

'He's funny, he is. Fancy meeting a cat who looks like a kitten and talks like a grown-up.'

'Out of my way,' I meowed, pushing them apart.

'You're peculiar enough to join our gang. What d'ya think, Zorb? Shall we make him a member?'

'If he wants, he can.' Zorba turned to me. 'You want to join our gang, "Le Freak"?'

'Dream on!' I meowed, striding off.

'We'll make you an honorary member,' Zorba called out.

12

Should have kept my big mouth shut!

'Jodie,' I called from her window ledge, waving a paw to get her attention.

Jodie didn't see or hear me. Her legs were thrown over the arm of her swivel chair. She was scribbling something on a pad.

I hopped down on the carpet and took a good look at her. She'd washed her hair. It was plaited and bound with cord. She was wearing a clean T-shirt with 'Save the Dolphins' written on it. Maybe it was just me, but she looked quite pretty. Her nose looked less pointed and ...

'Omzak, I was waiting and waiting,' Jodie said gleefully. She swung her legs back over the chair and bent down.

'High five,' she said, holding out her hand as if it was some sort of ritual I had to take part in.

'High five.' I tapped her palm with my paw. Then I shamed myself by burping again. 'Sorry, it's those sardines,' I said, checking my skin to see if I'd come out in a rash.

Jodie giggled. 'It's so funny listening to a kitten talk.'

'I'm glad you think it's funny,' I said, glancing at the book she'd been writing in. 'Homework?'

Jodie nodded. 'It's a story about David and Goliath and how David defeated a six-foot-nine warrior who wore heavy metal armour. David was just a little shepherd boy who didn't have any proper weapons.'

'David killed Goliath with a stone from his sling that went straight through the giant's forehead like a bullet.'

'You know everything,' Jodie said.

I nodded. What was the point of being modest?

Jodie looked round my back, as if I was hiding something. 'Did you bring my magnetosphere?'

'It's not finished. Zorba's gone to Maccles to do some detective work.'

'Maccles? What detective work?' Jodie twiddled with her plaits.

'His uncle's gone missing,' I said.

Jodie blinked rapidly. 'Maccles is where Horacio was going.'

'How d'you know?' I said.

'Because when he wants to tell me something, he taps the floor with his paw. Then he stretches his mouth like he's yawning.' Jodie showed me. 'If he's going Maccles way, he twitches his right ear.' She tugged her right plait. 'And if he's going to see friends in Minchin, he twitches his left ear.'

'You just interpreted it like that,' I said.

'No, I know everything he wants to tell me. One time when he didn't come back after two days I saw him in a dream. He'd been in an accident and I knew he was in Minchin because he'd twitched his left ear – so my dad took me there.'

'And then what?' I said.

'Horacio was at the vet's. With his head bandaged.'

'Just coincidence,' I said.

'No, my mum calls me the cat whisperer – and I'm starting to get scared because last night I saw Horacio in another dream. He was locked up in something round – like a biscuit tin – and he was scratching trying to get out … I could hear trains going past.' Jodie stood and walked to the window. 'I've got a horrible feeling,' she said, looking down the street. 'Now I remember – in my dream, there were two horrible creatures wearing hoods.'

'When Zorba gets back, I'll ask him what he knows,' I said, cutting Jodie short because she was getting upset.

Jodie was quiet for a few minutes. She looked so deep in thought, I didn't dare speak.

'Omzak,' Jodie said. 'Out of all the children on Earth, why did your ruler pick me?'

There was no way I was going to tell her she hadn't been chosen. Or that I'd been kicked out of Catopia for the same reason she'd been suspended from school. 'He must have had his reasons,' I said.

Jodie scratched a scab on her nose. 'Wonder what they were.'

'Dunno,' I said, pointing to a framed photo of her sitting on a man's lap. 'I'm guessing that's your dad. Is he away working somewhere?'

Jodie scowled. The blotches on her face spread to her neck. 'I haven't got a dad!' She picked up the photo and threw it on the floor. Bits of glass bounced over the carpet. 'Don't know why I kept that stupid picture.' She stamped on the frame, threw herself on her bed and started sobbing.

'I think I'd better go,' I said, wishing I hadn't brought the subject up.

She sat up and glared at me, her eyes red from crying. 'Yes, you'd better.' She threw a stuffed dolphin at me. 'I know why your ruler sent you. It's because he felt sorry for me, but I don't need you, or anyone.'

13

Getting blamed for everything

Zorba must have guessed by the look on my face I was in a bad mood.

'Don't dare talk to me,' I meowed, to make sure he didn't.

He was standing upright, forepaws pressed against the wall. 'I'm doing the exercise to learn to stand up. Watch how good I have become,' he meowed.

Huffing, because I couldn't care less, I watched him push himself away from the wall. He threw his forepaws in the air. 'Look!' he called, losing his balance as soon as the word was out. His belly hit the wall with a thud. 'Two exercises in one. Soon my stomach will be strong as iron. Good, eh?'

I kicked the rickety chair out of the way and dragged the three-legged table to the side. 'I said don't talk!'

I limbered up with a hundred press-ups, did a bit of tai chi to calm my mind and followed this with some karate exercises. From mid-air splits, I back-flipped to the ground, did a couple of somersaults and balanced on one paw.

'What you are doing is incredible,' Zorba meowed.

I jumped to my feet and brushed myself down. 'I've been doing that since I was six months old.'

Zorba, walking like a clothes peg, took a few steps up on his hind legs then gave up and lumbered towards me on all fours. 'You were like Kung Fu Panda,' he meowed.

I had no idea who Kung Fu Panda was but there was no way any panda was up to my standard.

'You were like Top Cat and Tarzan and…'

I never got to hear who else because his sentence was interrupted by Pasha. 'And what d'you call this?' she hissed, trotting into the yard. She'd grown so much fur, she looked like a giant ball of fluff.

Pasha lifted a forepaw, pushed back the fur hanging over her eyes and gave me a murderous look. 'I've got so much new hair I look like a sheepdog.'

I held back a nervous laugh. 'It's your fault for making me spill the herbs and muddle up the proportions.'

'What tom in his right mind would be interested in me now?' Pasha hissed.

Zorba wiggled his eyebrows at her.

'No, Zorba, I wouldn't go out with you, even if elephants could fly,' she meowed, turning to smoulder at me. 'And you should be ashamed of yourself.'

'Serves you right,' I meowed to her back as she stomped off, fur trailing the ground. 'Whoever invented the word vain, invented it to describe you.' I gave the rickety chair a kick. 'I'm not letting my day end like this. I'm going back to Jodie's.'

14

The piano competition

'My ruler didn't send me to you because he felt sorry for you. He didn't even know about whatever it was your dad did,' I said to Jodie.

'Why did he then?' she said, her head turned away from me.

I decided to come clean. 'I got into a fight, which Leorio thought was a threat to Catopia's safety, and he sent me here as a punishment,' I said.

'No!' Jodie said, forgetting to be mad and patting the duvet so I could sit down next to her. 'Have you been banished forever?' She sneezed.

I jumped on the end of her bed so I wouldn't be contaminated by her germs. 'When he thinks I've stopped being arrogant, I'll be allowed to go back,' I said.

'What are you supposed to do here?' Jodie said.

'To live like an Earth cat, become a pet and make myself useful,' I said. 'But like you don't want to talk about your dad, I don't want to talk

71

about that. Why don't we test each other on history or something?'

'It's a shame you don't play piano or we could have a competition to see who plays best.'

'That wouldn't be much of a competition because I'm definitely best,' I said.

'What, you mean you can play piano?' Jodie's eyes widened. 'That's … *amazing*.'

'Music's on our curriculum at nursery school,' I said, wondering what all the fuss was about.

'I could bring up the tray table from the living room. We could put the piano stool on top of that.'

'No way,' I said. 'I'm not making myself look stupid.'

'You don't know how to play, that's why,' Jodie said.

'Then how come I've got ten trophies?'

'Prove it,' she said.

I was starting not to like Jodie again. She was sitting there with her arms crossed, like she was something special and I was a liar.

'All right, loser – I'll play you my new composition,' I said. 'But if you laugh …'

'I won't laugh.' Jodie was on her feet faster than a ferret. She brought the tray table up and put the stool on top. 'I'll hold the legs while you jump on.'

I somersaulted onto it. This was war and I was going to win.

'That was clever,' Jodie said.

'*That* was peanuts,' I said, stretching my hind legs out. I pressed them against the piano lid and slid to and fro to see how it felt. 'You understand that because of size, I won't be able to reach every note?'

Jodie nodded. 'Do what you can.'

I took a deep breath and closed my eyes.

Within seconds I'd mastered the art of sliding across the keyboard like a skater on ice. My front paws flew over the notes. My head bobbed. My tail banged against the stool, keeping time. I got so lost in my brilliance, I forgot where I was. When I opened my eyes, I jumped with surprise to see Jodie leaning over me.

'Wow,' she said, looking around her room as though what she'd just witnessed couldn't be real. 'That was *amazing*. Especially the bit when you jumped on the keyboard and started banging notes with your head.'

I squirmed with red-hot embarrassment, unable to believe I'd behaved like some loony. 'Another example of the humbleness I'm learning,' I said, coughing into my paw.

'You play piano better than the most famous composers. I could imagine pieces of glacier ice breaking into the sea – I could see dolphins jumping through the waves, then an angry storm, then I could see wings flapping and a purple sky.'

73

I shrugged my shoulders. 'When you're the best, you're the best,' I said.

'Can I play it – the way I heard it in my mind?' Jodie said, dancing about in excitement.

'You'd better not mess it up,' I said. I leapt on top of the piano and watched Jodie push the tray table out of the way. She made herself comfortable on the stool and rested her fingers on the keys. 'What I think,' she said, forehead furrowed in concentration, 'is instead of starting where you did, it could start like this.'

The next moment, her fingers struck the first notes and I couldn't take my eyes off her. Until then, all I'd seen was a gangly girl who, when she wasn't flopping about the place, sat with her shoulders scrunched up.

'And then,' Jodie said, looking up at me, 'what if we make this bit faster?' Her fingers hit the keys again and she was off like a horse galloping through the wind.

There was no way of getting away from it. Jodie was nearly as talented as me.

She stopped playing mid-stream to study the keyboard as if it was a game of chess. Brushing the hair off her face with the back of her arm, she looked at me again.

'And this could be the finale.' She tinkled various notes with the tips of her fingers until she'd built the

74

sound to a crescendo. Then, with a grand flourish, she swept her hands across the keys. 'Can I play it at the Pavilion? I'll write both our names on the composition.'

I'd struck gold. I'd go down in history as the first Catopian who'd had his music played at a famous venue since we'd left Earth. I was bound to get a medal for that when I got back home. 'Yeah, all right,' I said.

'So who's the winner?' Jodie clapped her hands.

If I hadn't played at a disadvantage, I'd have said me, but since she was going to play at the Pavilion I decided to be fair. 'Let's call it a tie,' I said.

'High five,' Jodie said.

I tapped her palm with my paw. 'High five.'

15

Blackmail

When I got back to the yard, Zorba was admiring himself in a mirror. His coat was so shiny it looked as if he'd blacked it with polish.

'Find out any more about the cat snatchers?' I asked.

'They are nowhere in Maccles. A friend told me he thinks they have moved again.' Zorba gave a fed-up sigh, as if the kidnappers should do everyone a favour by staying put in one place.

'No other clues?' I meowed.

'No. But I have sent out a bigger search party. By tomorrow I am sure we will track them down.'

If there is anyone to track down, I thought, watching Zorba wink at his reflection.

'And what do you think about this?' Zorba turned to show me how well he'd groomed himself.

'I'm starting not to know you,' I meowed in encouragement. 'Oh, and by the way, Jodie's worried something's happened to her cat.'

'What's his name?' Zorba meowed, blowing himself a kiss in the mirror.

'Horacio.'

Zorba shook his head. 'Doesn't hang out with us.'

'Oh well, I asked. Is the magnetosphere ready?'

'I will collect the parts on my way back from the party,' Zorba replied, 'then I will finish it and give it to you.'

'What party?'

'The triplets are throwing a party in their garden – you should come along.'

I looked across at the coal bunker. 'No thanks. I'll stay here and read the books on ancient Greece you came across.'

'No, you must come. You must bring some fun into your life.' Zorba clicked his claws like he was ready to break into dance.

'I don't do parties,' I said.

'But Pasha insists. When she came back here, she said I must take care of you because…'

'Yeah, I know. She thinks I'm crazy,' I interrupted.

Zorba patted his belly, which sounded hollow. Enjoying the sound, he patted it again. 'The way she looked at me today, I think she was seeing a love god,' he meowed, slicking back the fur on his head.

'Whatever she was seeing, you're going to the party on your own,' I meowed.

Zorba lowered his face, pulled his chin in and

turned his head sideways. 'Then maybe I have more important things to do, than finishing magneto-spheres.'

'That's blackmail!'

'What do you have to lose?' Zorba meowed, still avoiding my eyes. 'We go for one hour, I'll fix Jodie's bracelet and then you can go where you want.'

'I'm not being bullied by Pasha,' I objected.

Zorba scratched his belly. 'I think your ruler would want you to come. How can you say you have lived with Earth cats if you don't hang out with us?'

'I've never been to a party and I'm not lowering myself to go to an Earth cat one.'

'Let me get a dictionary to see what the real meaning of humbleness is,' Zorba meowed, turning towards the coal bunker.

I dragged him back by the tail. 'By the time you've found it, it'll be midnight,' I meowed. 'Oh, all right, I'll come – but don't get me involved in anything.'

16

Incident of the feral cat gatecrashers

The party in the triplets' garden was in full swing when we got there. It was a wealthier part of Mapulsbury than where Jodie lived. This garden had stone statues and a fountain in the middle of the lawn. For the buffet, two frozen salmons had been thrown on a slab, next to which sat a tub of clotted cream.

'How many calories does a lick of cream have?' Zorba asked.

'Couldn't care less,' I meowed. I looked round for somewhere to sit, as far away from the rowdiness as possible.

In the far corner of the patio was a recliner covered in expensive palm tree fabric. It had an umbrella to match. I could pretend I was on a desert island and the hour would pass in a flash. I marched over, jumped on and placed my forepaws behind my head.

The first thing I'll have for dinner when I get back to Catopia is caviar and a chocolate milkshake.

I was imagining the tastes when the sound of someone meowing my name brought me back from my fantasy. I didn't even need to look to know who it was.

'Ommmmmmmzakkkkkk,' Floss meowed again.

I managed a fake smile.

'What?' I said.

'I'll come and keep you company in a while, lovey.'

I shrugged my shoulders, hoping my time would be up before that came about, and turned my attention to Zorba. He'd reappeared on the lawn and was trying to walk upright. After managing a few steps, he started to wobble and was about to collapse when Floss grabbed his tail.

'Up, up, up. Think "I'm a love god", ducks,' Floss meowed like he was singing an opera.

Zorba rose to full height, gave Floss a thumbs-up sign and continued to stumble around the fountain.

'That's it, lovey,' Floss shrilled, flouncing along behind in his stupid pink tutu.

Suddenly, the music from *Swan Lake* blared out from loudspeakers.

Floss ecstatically clasped his paws, bent his knees, then leapt in the air like a gazelle.

'Pull my tail tighter,' Zorba meowed, starting to topple. Thinking Floss was still there, Zorba regained his balance. 'Now I've got it,' Zorba meowed.

You're such a klutz, I thought. I glanced at Floss, who was twirling on his toes. *And there is an even bigger klutz.* What tom in his right mind would want to be seen in a ballet skirt?

Unable to make sense of it, I looked to see what other entertainment was on offer. On a first-floor balcony, three cats were playing makeshift instruments. The first was blowing through straws like they were trumpets; the second was drumming a tin with chopsticks. The third was using metal bottle tops as cymbals.

One thing was sure, Earth cats had evolved. I sat up to get a proper look. As I did, the pong of something vile went up my nose.

I leaned over the recliner and sniffed. The smell reminded me of bad breath and urine. My nose led me to a hedge on the other side of the garden.

Six feral cats, crawling low on their stomachs, were squeezing their way underneath. Their lips were drawn back to show their teeth. One had clumps of fur missing, one had ripped ears, and another was so battered, there was a flat patch where its nose had been.

I stood up and waved at the triplets to warn them. They were skipping along the washing line, balancing apples on their heads.

Floss was on another planet, flapping his arms like a swan.

Zorba was wobbling around the fountain with his back towards me.

I wanted to scream, 'Can't you smell the stink?' With one paw I clamped my nostrils shut. With the other I scratched my ruff.

The feral cats' ears were pricked back and they pawed at the earth like angry bulls. Growling, they broke into a run and took off full pelt across the lawn, swiping and slashing out with their claws at anything in their way. It wasn't long before the air filled with distraught meows and hedges rustled with the sound of deserters.

Bloody-nosed and yelping, a cat flew over my head to make its escape.

'Coward,' I meowed, looking to see which cats hadn't been scared off.

The only ones left were Floss, the triplets and Zorba.

Floss was entangled with two of the attackers, under a muddle of fur. He brandished his paws like boxing gloves. I watched him sock one on the nose then slam his fist in the other one's gut. I was thinking that maybe I'd judged him too fast when one of the ferals ripped his tutu and Floss ran off squealing like a sissy.

Two of the triplets were battling it out in a tug of war, with a salmon as the rope.

They had its head in their mouths and they

struggled to drag it their way. At the tail end, two ferals were trying to tug it back. Apart from a lot of hissing, no one was winning. The only real action came from Threesy. He was running along the washing line, pelting the thieves with biscuits.

My eyes darted back to Zorba to see how he was getting on.

The feral with no nose had attached itself to his shoulders and was digging its teeth in his neck. Zorba was bucking like a rodeo horse, trying to throw him off. A black and white feral with scraggy fur had launched a claw-your-face-off attack, Zorba's ear was trickling with blood.

Zorba took a swipe and scratched his opponent's eye. The feral yowled and ran off. 'Good going, Zorba,' I meowed.

Not knowing who to watch, I turned to Floss, who was ducking and dodging like a ballerina to keep two ferals at bay.

The triplets were swinging the feral cat with no ear round like an aeroplane. His partner in crime was tucking into a salmon.

Zorba's frantic meows reached my ears. I spun round to see both attackers back in play. They were meowing in amusement because they'd stuck a plastic bag over his head. While Zorba furiously scratched at it, they kept twisting the ends. It was as tight as a gas mask.

I wanted to shout, *'Use your forepaws to reach back and punch them in the groin. Use your hind legs and give them a mule kick.'*

The ferals pressed the bag over Zorba's mouth. He stopped scratching at the plastic. His paws went limp. He slumped forwards and stayed there.

I waited five seconds.

No movement.

Ten seconds.

Still no movement.

After I've saved him, I'm going to throttle him, I thought, backflipping to his rescue.

I flew at Zorba's attackers, my tail swishing like a sword, and landed a blow to the first cat's head. Kicking out with all fours, I whacked the second in the stomach and tossed it in the air. When they came at me again, I spun myself in a cone, landing blow after blow with my tail and paws.

In thirty seconds flat, one lay in a heap at my feet and the other was dangling from a branch.

I pulled the bag off Zorba's face and slapped him on the back.

'It's you,' Zorba wheezed. 'I thought I'd never see your face again.'

'You owe me big time,' I meowed, furious that I'd ended up in an Earth cat brawl.

'How are the others doing?' Zorba meowed, trying to focus his eyes.

'If they don't know how to defend themselves, that's their problem.'

Zorba looked dolefully at Floss and back at me. 'You're right. What does Floss need a tail for anyway?'

Still annoyed, I turned to see what Zorba was on about.

Floss was twisted in a knot, trying to retrieve his tail from the mouth of a feral. A second feral had its teeth around Floss's ear, about to bite it off.

Before I'd had time to think, I'd somersaulted over to the trouble spot, kicked the ear thief off Floss's head and sent him spiralling like a rocket. I jumped on the other feral's back, karate-chopped his neck and yanked Floss's tail free.

'Thanks, captain, I'll take it from here,' Floss meowed, striking his attacker's nose.

I whirled round to see two ferals making off with the salmons. 'Stop, thieves!' I meowed. With a triple somersault, I landed on their shoulders and rode them like sled dogs until I'd slowed them down.

'Drop the fish,' I meowed, pulling them up by their ears.

The ferals dropped it. They looked up to see who was ordering them about.

'And next time there's a party, wait until you're invited.' I smacked their heads together. 'Now take your friends and get out.'

Looking stupefied, the feral cats stared at me.

'What kind of kitten are *you*?'

'Now!' I meowed.

'Who d'ya think you are, squirt face?' one of them said, having the nerve to growl.

'I'll show you.' I nabbed it by its tail, span on the spot and tossed it over the hedge.

A scalded *'Meeeoooooow!'* rang out. Then came a rustling of leaves, followed by silence.

At the gate, the other feral cats turned, their eyes glinting with rage. 'We'll get you back,' they growled.

I folded my forearms across my chest to let them know I couldn't care less. 'You and whose army?' I meowed, waving them off.

When I turned, the triplets were gazing at me with shock and admiration. Floss was cooing as if he'd died and gone to heaven, and Zorba was sobbing with emotion.

'I am lucky you came so I could take care of you.' Zorba threw himself at my legs and clung to them.

'Get a grip. Remember you're a grown-up,' I meowed.

'You *have* to teach me to fight like you,' Floss meowed, dipping the tip of his tail in the fountain to cool it off. 'Just look what those nasty brutes did to my tutu.' He held out a tattered strip of skirt.

'I think my hour's up,' I meowed, shaking off Zorba's paws.

'I will tell my children about the Catopian I love like a brother.' Zorba lifted his eyes to the sky. 'Omzak, who taught me how to be a love god, who taught me how to do martial arts.'

'I never said I'd teach you martial arts,' I meowed.

The triplets surrounded me, re-enacting the moves I'd used to defeat the ferals. 'You're even better than James Bond. We wanna learn those fancy moves.'

'Three cheers for Omzak,' shrilled Floss.

'Hip, hip, hooray!' they chorused together.

I covered my ears with my paws. 'See you back at the yard.'

17

I can hear them plotting

The first thing I did when I got back to Zorba's was to scrub off the stink of the ferals that had worked its way into my fur. I was so mad I felt like steam was coming out of my ears. I took a pile of cans inside the bunker and smacked them at the walls.

Outside Zorba, Floss and the triplets were whispering, but I could still hear every word. They were plotting how to persuade me to teach them martial arts.

I marched out. 'How much longer you gonna be with that?' I meowed, watching Zorba screw a part into the magnetosphere.

'Nearly done,' Zorba meowed.

Bongo, the cat that had been playing the tin with chopsticks, came dashing into the yard looking hot and bothered.

'Those kidnappers have come to Mapulsbury. I stopped to say hi to Stallone. He said he saw them,' he squeaked.

Zorba's ears shot up. 'When?' he meowed.

'About three in the morning he was sitting at his window and saw two really creepy types. One had some sort of a gun and the other had a big lump under his cape.'

Zorba turned to me. 'It sounds like the people I told you about.'

'Then you need to organise yourselves and do something about it,' I meowed.

Zorba puckered his lips. 'I was thinking maybe ...'

I pointed to my lips. 'NO.'

'Without you I would be dead,' Zorba said.

'It's a miracle you've lasted this long!'

'Which is why you must train us in warfare,' Zorba insisted.

The triplets saluted. Floss clasped his paws. 'We'd never be scared of bullies again, Captain Omzak.'

'No,' I meowed. 'Leave me out of this.'

Zorba solemnly shook his head. 'One day when you are eating curry, remember it could be me.'

I tried to shake off the image of Zorba with his head inside a plastic bag. I knew that if the kidnappers were real and got hold of him, he wouldn't stand a chance.

'A long time ago your ancestors were Earth cats,' Zorba meowed. 'Why do you think you are better than us?'

I snatched the magnetosphere. 'You've got to

be the most pathetic cat in the universe. Oh, all right.'

Floss fanned his nose with his tail. 'This is the best day of my life,' he meowed.

'Don't dare turn up in a ballet skirt or you're out,' I meowed.

The triplets approached. 'Thanks a million, guv.'

'You're to call me Captain Omzak,' I meowed.

'Got it, guv,' they meowed.

I gave them the look I used when I wanted to make things clear.

They jumped on their hind legs and saluted. 'Got it, Captain Omzak.'

'That's more like it.'

I looked at Zorba. His eyes were raised to heaven in a prayer of thankfulness.

I prodded him. 'Where do you want your training session?'

'In the woods near the mushroom patch.'

'I don't know how you talked me into this but while I'm gone don't even think about sleeping,' I meowed. 'Practise every move you've seen me do.'

'I will begin as soon as you leave,' Zorba said.

'Good,' I meowed, marching off. 'We'll start at eight – sharp.'

18

On the trail of the catnappers

Jodie was propped up in bed reading when I slipped through her window.

'Omzak! I've been waiting hours for you to come back,' she whined.

'Ssh.' I put a paw to my lips. 'Where's your mother?'

'She's in bed. It's past ten o'clock,' Jodie whispered. 'But she can't hear us from her bedroom.'

Throwing off her duvet, she ran to the piano and took a music sheet from the stand. 'Look, it says "Composition by Omzak the Catopian and Jodie Walkman".'

'Yeah, great,' I said, pulling the magnetosphere out of my pouch. I snapped it on her wrist.

Jodie brought it to her ear and listened to it tick. 'This is cool.' She pointed to a miniature Minnie Mouse sticker under the glass. 'Who thought of that?'

'Zorba. Who else?'

'I want to meet him to say thank you,' Jodie said, holding back a sneeze.

'You'll regret it,' I said, wishing I'd never set eyes on him.

'Are you all right? You seem very cross.'

'*Cross* doesn't come close to the way I feel,' I said.

'Why?'

'Because,' I huffed, 'I got talked into going to an Earth cat party.'

'I didn't know cats had parties,' Jodie said. 'I wish I'd been there.'

'I wish I hadn't,' I said. 'I ended up in a brawl with a bunch of stinky feral gatecrashers.'

'No!' Jodie sat up cross-legged on her bed. 'How did that happen?'

'I don't want to talk about it, but the result was I ended up promising to teach Zorba and his friends how to defend themselves.' I tugged my whiskers. '*Me*. A space cat warrior.'

'That was humble. Leorio will be very proud,' Jodie said.

'I couldn't care less whether he's proud or not. He's not the one training a bunch of misfits.'

'When are you training them?' Jodie asked.

'Tomorrow morning,' I said.

Jodie cupped her hands over her mouth. I knew what she was thinking before she said it. ' Can I come and watch? It's Saturday tomorrow.

My homework's done for when I go back to school.'

'Sorry, I've got enough on my plate. In any case, having a human watching will put them off.'

'I won't – you keep forgetting I understand cats. And I can bring some food for when they have their break.'

I glared at her. 'They won't be having a break!'

'Being so bad-tempered can make you sick you know, Omzak.' Jodie sneezed to prove it.

'Anyway, I'd better go,' I said.

'Where to?'

'To check a few things out.'

'Can you come back afterwards? I want to tell you something you made me understand.' She twiddled with the sleeve of her pyjamas. 'I don't mind what time it is. I'll leave the window open.'

'Can't it wait?' I said.

'It's something important,' she said.

'Oh, all right,' I said. 'But if you're asleep I'm not waking you up.'

19

Left for dead

I didn't mind the chill that came with the change of weather. The whistling wind, together with the river slapping against the bank, had a welcome mind-numbing effect. A walk in the fields was just what I needed. The smell of bluebells under my paws. Frogs croaking their news and hopping to and fro – without trying to get me involved in their lives.

I plucked a violet, sniffed it and shook my head. I was still in shock that I'd agreed to train Zorba and his friends. And *now* I was trekking to a train station in the dead of night to check out … what?

Zorba's crazy theory about strange men who kidnapped cats to put them in casseroles?

Jodie's surreal dream where hooded creatures held cats hostage in biscuit tins?

I quickened my step and turned left along the riverbank.

In the distance I could hear the rumble of wheels.

Following my instincts, I marched towards a makeshift bridge and crossed over. A path to my right took me to the train station. It looked like a ghost town. The waiting room door was banging on its hinges, the walls were covered in graffiti, and the place stank of beer and mouldy pizzas.

I watched a bucket, driven by the wind, bounce its way along the tracks. *This is going to prove a waste of time,* I thought, jumping down and walking over the tracks.

A cloud of dust blew up my nose as I stepped on the platform. Shielding my eyes, I spluttered into my paws. My tail started jumping of its own accord – a sure danger signal.

I sniffed the air and picked up a scent I recognised. It wasn't mouldy food or beer … And it was getting stronger.

It was too dark to see properly, but at the end of the platform was a cluster of glittery specks. The hairs on my ruff bristled.

I glanced up at the waiting room roof to see a pair of fierce eyes trained on me. Straight away, I knew. The stink was bad breath and urine. It was the gatecrashing ferals I'd done battle with at the triplets' party.

Tail whirling like a helicopter blade, I rose up on my hind legs, rolled my paws into fists and counted the cats creeping stealthily closer.

To my left, three pairs of eyes glowed like lumps of burning coal.

To my right were two sets of snapping teeth.

All around was the sound of hissing.

'This time you're really getting it,' I meowed, ready to whack the feral hurtling at me. It landed on my head. I struck hard and sent it flying across the tracks. I whipped a second cat with my tail and batted it down the platform. Three more ferals rushed at me from behind, growling like tigers.

'You're getting on my nerves,' I meowed. Lashing out with my paws and claws, I beat two of them to pulp. As they dropped at my feet, I rammed my head in the third one's gut.

Five down.

I looked up at the roof just as an approaching train flashed its headlamps. In their glow, I saw the sixth gang member flying down like a bat. Its claws were out, ready to rip into me.

At the last moment, I backflipped out of the way. The feral crashed on the platform. There was a *thump* as his nose hit the concrete.

There was the thunderous roar of wheels and *whoo-whoo* of a whistle as the train approached. I glanced up at the roof again.

Yet another cat had climbed on. Growling deep from its belly, it threw something.

Roof slates rained down on me like bombs. As I

ducked and dodged the avalanche, I fought off a feral that had come at me out of nowhere. A slate skimmed my shoulders. Another bounced off my tail. I lifted my paws to protect my head. CRR-AACK. Something sharp sliced into my skull.

A feral kicked me in the back. As I fell forwards, I heard it meow, 'That's squirt face taught.' Something sticky was running down my eyes. I had the sensation I was falling. I closed my eyes against the dazzling light and crashed on the train tracks. A shard of glass sliced into my gut. My body went into a spasm. I tried to roll to safety, but my limbs wouldn't move. My teeth rattled. The weight of the train shook the tracks.

'Whoo-whoo. Whoo-whoo.'

I threw myself at the wall, felt the explosion as my head made contact, saw a kaleidoscope of colours …

… and blacked out.

20

The giant saucer

When my eyes flickered open, I didn't know where I was. It was pitch black. I was sprawled on my stomach and my head felt like a lead block. I followed the dots moving in and out like waves. They were the eyes of rats. Dozens of them.

I forced myself to sit up. My bones felt like they'd been smashed with a mallet. *No way the ferals are getting away with what they've done.* I inched my way towards the ladder. *If it takes all night, I'll find them.* I dragged myself up and fell on the platform.

Everything was blurry.

Buildings swayed.

Trees looked like waltzing phantoms.

The bump on my head was the size of a conker. Where the glass had gone into my stomach, I was bleeding. I spat out the taste of rust and sniffed. *Which way have the ferals gone?*

Their scent led me into a forest. The smell of urine was fresh, as if they'd wet themselves from fright. I pressed a leaf to my stomach to stem the bleeding. Limping at a snail's pace, I went to investigate. The claw marks etched into the earth and the clumps of broken bracken suggested the ferals had been taken by force.

They've been kidnapped. The people Zorba talked about do exist.

I wiped a dribble of blood off my mouth. I wondered whether I was concussed and would wake up at the vet's and see Jodie standing there. *This is too weird,* I thought, forcing myself on.

The feral cats' scent led to a dried-up lake overhung with trees. I couldn't see any cats. Or the kidnappers. I focused carefully because my sight was still blurry. Either it was a mirage or a giant saucer covered the whole area of the lake. There were twigs scattered on top to camouflage it.

Slipping and sliding, I fell down the bank. I could hear muffled caterwauling.

Jodie's words came back to me. *'Horacio was scratching, and it sounded like he was in a biscuit tin.'* Except it wasn't a tin, it was a … SPACESHIP.

I picked up a stick and scraped the dirt from a window. There were so many cats packed inside, they couldn't move. The howling was pitiful. Those closest to the walls scratched at them like maniacs. Horacio, whom I recognised from Jodie's photo, was throwing himself at a window. Through the crush of bodies, I saw the ferals. They were squashed together by the door.

What is a spaceship doing on Earth? Why are aliens kidnapping cats?

I crawled around the door. It was thicker than a tank. *Who does the spaceship belong to? I need to find them to steal the remote control.*

I clambered back down and threw up. I felt weak from loss of blood but *no way* was I giving up. The wind sent up the unmistakable scent of rotting meat...

They were VARIANS! The ape-like creatures that lived on the other side of our boundary line. *What were they up to?* My eyes picked up a finger of light. It was coming from a hut. All the windows except one were blacked out with paper.

I crawled there on my stomach, took a deep breath and grabbed the window ledge. I peered through the crack. *It couldn't be!* It was SKABBART.

It has to be a billion to one chance that we are both in Mapulsbury.

I hauled myself on the ledge, held the wall for support and looked in again.

Skabbart and another Varian were at a table eating. And Skabbart looked uglier than ever. A candle was shining on his face, making his ears seem monstrously big, his fangs extraordinarily long, and his eyes bulge like purple ping-pong balls.

100

I watched him chew a worm, slime dripping off his chin. *When Leorio said to me 'look for ways to make up for what you've done', was this what he meant?*

Skabbart clumped around the room, scratching his belly like a Sumo wrestler. 'I say we head to that uninhabited planet Dimp and get our brainwashing programme started.'

'Whatever you say,' Dimp said. He had the eyes, ears and fangs of a Varian but they were softer. He looked so innocent, I wondered how Skabbart had persuaded him to take part in his evil scheme. Dimp picked out a worm from the crawling mass He was about to put it in his mouth when Skabbart snatched it.

'Yes, we'll hunt one more time – just for fun – then leave,' Skabbart said, throwing the worm down his throat. He cracked his knuckles. 'We have enough cats to build our army.'

My heart flipped. *Why is he building an army?*

'If that scumbag Omzak hadn't butted in,' Skabbart said, picking up a raw potato and spearing it with his fangs, 'I'd have been able to steal Leorio's crown. It would have brought a good price.'

I shook with outrage. As soon as I got my strength back I was going to build a bonfire and watch his carcass shrivel to ash.

'I don't think you would have, Captain Skabbart,'

Dimp said. 'Leorio must have known you were there.'

Skabbart dug his talons into the edge of the table. 'Are you saying I didn't know what I was doing?' His purple eyes turned crimson. He spat the potato at the wall.

'No, no. I meant this new plan of yours is a billion times better. It's the work of a genius, a mastermind.' He offered Skabbart a strawberry.

Wrinkling his snout, Skabbart waved it away. 'So you believe I'll be Catopia's new ruler?'

'Definitely,' Dimp gushed.

'Soon I'll have everything I ever wanted' Skabbart sighed

Dimp gave his snout a rub.'You did mean it when you said I'd be your second in command?' he asked uncertainly.

'As long as you prove worthy.' Skabbart dug his talons into Dimp's shoulders.

Dimp winced from the pain. 'You'll see when we go to Fos,' he squeaked

Skabbart thumped round the hut, his tail throwing up dust as it smacked the floor. 'How I'm looking forward to that.'

Fos? My whiskers twitched uncontrollably. That was the planet where I'd first met Skabbart and chased him off for trying to steal their priceless mineral. Not content with trying to blow up

Catopia, he planned to go back there and wreak havoc...

Skabbart snorted like a pig, twiddling with the tufts of hair on his head. 'I can see it all now. Caskets and caskets of Fosiancrystals. A four-poster bed made of twenty-two carat gold – a spaceship with a jacuzzi.' Skabbart chortled. 'And I think I'll make Omzak my personal slave.'

If I hadn't felt so weak, I'd have gone in and bashed his brains in.

'From what you've told me, though, isn't Omzak an upstart?' Dimp said.

'When I've finished with him he won't be an upstart because after I've used my serum to brainwash the cats in the spaceship – I'm going to... to...' Skabbart started braying like a demented hyena. He held on to the table until he'd brought himself under control. 'I'm going to destroy Omzak's brain with it,' Skabbart spluttered.

A wave of delirium swept over me. *Did Skabbart's madness know no end?*

'A serum?' Dimp said, wiping his face with a rag.

Skabbart slapped him on the shoulder. 'I'd never use it on *you*, if that's what you're thinking. I promised you half my wealth.'

If Dimp had seen the hostile glint in his eyes, he'd have known Skabbart was a cheating, scheming, vile liar.

My head banging like jungle drums, I eased myself to the ground. I had less than twenty-four hours to stop Skabbart in his tracks. And I barely had strength to crawl.

21

Devastated and defeated

I don't remember how I got back to Jodie's, how I climbed up the drainpipe or ended up on her bed.

One moment the ceiling looked like a ceiling, then like the lid of a box.

Jodie's voice kept coming in and out to the sound of two dogs barking and water running through pipes. I was icy cold and shivery, and my mind flashed with images of train tracks, spaceships and Skabbart's eyes.

'I know this stings but I need to put it on your bump.'

It was Jodie's voice again.

I could feel hands washing my fur in soapy water that smelled of peaches, then a bandage being wrapped round my head.

I had the sensation I was being rocked. I could hear Jodie's heart beating against my chest. Unsure whether I was asleep or awake, I licked away a tear.

'I can't believe what those feral cats did,' Jodie

sniffed. 'It's a good job you didn't find them when you went to look for them or you could have been dead by now.'

I gave a faint nod of my head.

'Or did you find them, like you said before?'

I shook my head, not sure what I'd told her and hadn't.

'And what about the men in the derelict hut? Did you find out who they are?'

'It was *Skabbart*,' I howled. 'Skabbart.'

I could feel Jodie's tears dripping down my ears.

'Who's Skabbart?' Jodie asked.

'The one I got in a fight with in Catopia'

'Don't cry, Omzak.'

Sounds I didn't recognise bubbled in my throat.

'Leorio was right. I'm arrogant,' I gurgled. 'I should have left him to deal with it. Look at the mess I've made.'

'You just got angry. When I'm angry, I do lots of stupid things,' Jodie said, stroking my paw. 'My dad tried to see me but I was so angry, I wanted to hurt him like he hurt me,' she said. 'I think it's fate you ended up with me.'

'I was too big for my boots, so I missed the clues you and Zorba gave me.'

'You were just upset because of your punishment,' Jodie said.

I snorted. 'I'm supposed to be a warrior – and a leader of others.'

'Tomorrow you'll lead Zorba and the others to … to victory,' Jodie said. 'You could make that your mantra.' Jodie sniffed. 'You remember you gave me a mantra asking for a best friend?' Her tears plopped off my chin.

I gave a nod, aware I was slipping into unconsciousness.

'Mine came true – because you're the best friend I've ever had.' She kissed my nose. 'And you're the best pet in the universe.'

22

Jodie threatens to go to the police

I woke up to see Jodie's tousled head beside mine on the pillow. My memory of the night before was muddled – I could only remember vague bits and pieces.

I rolled away and carefully stretched my paws. They were stiff as washing pegs. I sat up, wiggled them and lowered myself to the carpet. My hind paws were wobbly but no bones were broken. There was a bit of dried blood where the glass had pierced my gut. But that didn't hurt. The only pain was coming from my head. It felt like someone was banging a gong.

I lifted my forepaws, unwrapped the bandage and touched the bump. It had gone down to the size of a grape.

'Omzak?'

I turned to see Jodie sleepily rubbing her eyes. 'Are you feeling better?'

'Only thanks to you,' I said.

Jodie yawned and clambered out of bed. 'Are you well enough to teach Zorba and his friends martial arts?'

'Sure am.'

'That's great! Would you like cornflakes or apple pie for breakfast?' Jodie said, heading out of the bedroom.

'Apple pie,' I called out, glancing at the clock.

It was 7 a.m. The first thing on my agenda was to clean myself up. The wastebasket was full of muddy, bloodied paper – but on the bedside table was a bowl of clean water and a fresh flannel. Taking my time I climbed up, dipped the cloth in the bowl, wrung it out and gave my body a rub.

'After our cry last night, I feel much better,' Jodie said, putting a plate down on the bed. 'Do you?'

'I didn't cry,' I said. 'You must have been imagining things.'

I jumped down on the bed and broke off a piece of pie.

'Have you come up with a plan to beat Skabbart?' Jodie asked, cutting the pie into bite-size bits.

'I'm working on it,' I said, chewing hungrily. I'd had nothing to eat since the sardines.

'What can I do to help?' Jodie stood and pulled on a tracksuit.

I watched her tie her hair in a ponytail. 'Do you know anywhere that sells slings?'

'The toy shop in the high street,' Jodie said, rummaging in a drawer.

I swallowed the pie in my mouth. 'We'll need six. Do you have any money?'

Nodding, Jodie took out a pair of socks and threw them on the bed.

'Can you get hold of some rope and a roll of wire netting?' I asked.

'There's loads of rope in the garage and I know where to find netting,' she said, deciding which trainers to put on.

I tapped my lips, thinking about what else we'd need. 'And a sharp knife – and nails – the longest you can find.'

'There'll be some in my dad's toolbox.' Jodie grabbed a pad and made notes. 'And where in the woods will you be?'

'Near the mushroom patch.' I jumped down on the carpet, stood on my hind legs and limbered up with some stretches.

'Omzak,' Jodie said, 'before you go, I need to ask you something.'

'OK – but be quick. I need to catch Zorba before he leaves.' I did some press-ups, squirming in agony as the pain from my muscles shot down my tail.

'Last night, when you were confused, first you said you saw the missing cats, then you said you didn't. Now I want the truth. Did you see Horacio?'

I lifted my head and looked up. 'Yes,' I said, knowing she'd find out anyway.

Jodie's hand flew to her mouth. 'Where is he?' She blinked rapidly.

'In Skabbart's spaceship – in the dried-up lake,' I said, standing up and brushing myself down.

'In a ... SPACESHIP ...' Jodie sat open-mouthed, taking in what I'd said.

'Has he been tortured?'

'No, he's fine.'

Jodie threw her pad on the bed and scrambled to the floor. 'How did you find it?' she said, crossing her legs.

'I followed the feral cats' scent.'

Jodie nervously rocked back and forth. 'So you mean, after they beat you up, Skabbart found them and...'

'Threw them in the ship.' I flexed my forepaws to loosen them.

'Didn't you try to get in?' Jodie said.

'I need the remote control – Skabbart wears it on a belt round his waist.'

Jodie anxiously picked at her toes. 'I'm not letting Skabbart take Horacio back to – what's his planet called?'

'Varia.'

'To Varia?' Jodie pulled a face. 'Why does he want Earth cats anyway?'

'He's not taking them there,' I said, 'he's taking them to another planet to brainwash them.'

'Brainwash them!' Jodie gasped.

'To turn them into mafia cats and set them loose on Catopia,' I said, taking deep breaths to stay calm.

'Horacio doesn't want to be a brainwashed mafia cat.' Jodie vehemently shook her head. 'I'm not letting Skabbart do that. If Varians look like the creatures in my dream, they're horrid. When you go to rescue them, I'm coming.'

'No way,' I said.

'Horacio knows I know he's in trouble. If I don't help, he'll be upset.'

'Skabbart won't care that you're a child. He's a barbarian. Aside from the fact that you're too ill, you'll get killed.'

Jodie waved her wrist. She was still wearing the magnetosphere. 'I'm not ill. I'm cured. I haven't sneezed once since last night.'

'The answer's still no,' I said.

'I promise I won't get killed. Please? Please?'

'No,' I said.

Jodie defiantly crossed her arms. 'Fine then, but remember I know where the spaceship is, so you can let me come or I'll go on my own.'

'I'm not letting you run wild in the forest with a maniac on the prowl.'

'If you don't let me help, I'm going to the police.'

I knew Jodie meant it because she was fifty times more arrogant than me.

'OK. But you'd better obey orders and do everything I say.'

23

Preparing Zorba for the worst

When I got to Zorba's yard he was staring at an olive. His back was arched and he was making chirruping sounds, as if the olive was prey. Zorba pounced on it, batted it in the air and twisted on his back.

I sat down where I was, amazed at how fast Zorba transferred the olive to his back paws, shot it to his head and kicked it off his nose.

If his overnight transformation has been brought about by the shock of nearly dying yesterday, the lesson has been a good one.

Zorba jumped to his feet. Using his tail like a cricket bat he whacked an apple about. He chased it round the rickety chair, smacked it in the coal bunker and dived in after it.

I stared at the rusty tap, listening to it drip, and let my eyes wander round the yard. It was still shabby and untidy, but that hardly bothered me any more … *And what about Zorba?* When I first met him, all I'd seen was an overweight slob. Now I saw his heart was bigger than a skyscraper.

Zorba had got fed up of chasing fruit and come out of the bunker. He was hoisting his bulk up a drainpipe. Halfway up, he lost his grip and crashed to the ground with a heavy thump. 'Ooaaww,' he meowed, lying on his belly with his paws splayed out.

And he never cares how pathetic he looks!

I marched towards him. 'You OK?'

Zorba gave his head a shake, pushed himself up on all fours then stood. 'I am *very* fine.' Zorba saluted. He looked like a pirate because he was wearing a red spotted hankie round his head. 'Good morning, Capta...' Zorba stopped to stare at my bump, scratches and belly wound. He let out a long, sorry whistle. 'Pasha will kill me when she sees you!'

'Sit down, Zorba. I need to tell you something,' I meowed.

'Pasha has seen you already?'

'Just sit down,' I repeated. 'I've found the missing cats. Skabbart's the one who's been kidnapping them.'

'Skibbit? Where have I heard that name before ... You mean the one you call a scumbag? Are you saying he's here in ...?'

'Mapulsbury. He's hiding out in a hut near the train station and plans to take off tomorrow in the early hours.'

Zorba sat down, placed one paw on top of the other, then removed it to pat the ground. 'Do you think your ruler knew this?'

'I suspect so,' I meowed. 'I was so cocky I missed the clues.'

'What can you do? We all make mistakes,' Zorba sighed, staring into space. 'What I don't understand is why Skibbit is on Earth?'

'He's planning to brainwash the cats he kidnapped to turn them into soldiers to overthrow Catopia,' I explained.

Zorba fanned his whiskers. 'Overthrow Catopia?'

'Yeah, use them as shields. It would be a bloodbath because we'd have to shoot to defend our territory.'

'You mean … my Uncle Tickles could end up...' He opened his forepaws and mimicked being blasted through the head. 'BOOM?'

'Yes.'

'I am already confused. Start the story from the beginning,' Zorba meowed.

'I'll give you the details on the way to the woods, but to fast-track to the end, the cats are being held hostage in Skabbart's spaceship.'

One of Zorba's nostrils flared in astonishment. 'Po, po, po. I think I am having a nightmare.' Zorba pinched himself. 'No, it's real.'

'Very real,' I sighed.

Zorba adjusted his bandana. It had slipped down over his eyes. 'Before we go, I'd like to ask something. Because maybe I'll forget.'

I stood up because my muscles had gone to sleep. 'Go for it.' I walked up and down to ease the stiffness.

'Once, when we were talking, you said you hated Skabbart because of Fos. What did you mean when you said that?'

'I'll need to tell you a bit of history first.' I picked up an orange that was lying on the concrete and flicked it in the air with my tail. 'In my galaxy there are two planets. The one we share with the Varians and Fos. Fosians are peace loving creatures who wouldn't harm a scrubble.'

'A scrubble?' Zorba interrupted.

'Similar to an ant, let's say.'

Zorba nodded his nose at me. 'OK. Carry on the story.'

'Well, as I already mentioned, Varians stick to their own side and don't cause trouble – with the exception of one, that scumbag Skabbart.' I dribbled the apple like a football. 'Last year, I was with another warrior on space control duty and we were circling over Planet Fos when we saw Skabbart. He was dangling the leader of Fos by his legs and had a grenade in his other hand. Fortunately, we got Skabbart to back off, but he took off in a spaceship before we could arrest him.'

'Why was Skibbit there?' Zorba meowed, hugging his belly because it was rumbling.

'He was there trying to steal. The Fosians are guardians of a priceless mineral that looks like crystal. Myth has it these crystals are what brings light to stars.'

Zorba looked to the sky. There were no stars to see because it was morning, but he gazed up as if he was seeing them in the millions. 'Never will I look at a star again and not think about this. You know Fos means light in Greek, eh?' he meowed.

118

I nodded.

'Skibbit is a *bad* creature,' Zorba meowed. 'Let us go and get ready to fight him.'

24

Nightmare of turning Earth cats into warriors

Since there was no one around, we both marched upright through the woods; Zorba to practise his new skill and me to ease my leg muscles, which still felt stiffer than starch.

After I'd filled Zorba in with the details of what had happened the night before, we both fell into silence. I could hear Zorba clucking his tongue as if what I'd told him had given him the horrors. But facts had to be faced, even when they weren't nice.

There was a smell around me that reminded me of coconut. It was coming from a crop of gorse bushes. I sniffed it in to soothe my nerves and used the time to think through my battle plan. The first thing I had to do was convince my band of Earth cat warriors they were invincible, which, judging by Zorba's reaction, I'd gone about wrong.

I'll tell them about the mightiness of ants which, believing in their strength, can lift more than fifty times their weight. I'll point out that to ants, Varians would seem like giants but they wouldn't notice how ugly they were because … because …

'We're here,' Zorba meowed. He pulled his belly in, stuck out his chest and added a swagger to his step. 'And look – Pasha has come.'

Floss, wearing an orangey-green combat waistcoat, waved at me. 'Captain Ommmm-zakkkkkk,' he trilled. 'Can't wait to get started, ducks.'

The triplets saluted sharply. 'Morning, captain,' they chorused.

Pasha was hurrying towards me like a cat on a mission. She'd had a trim since the last time I'd seen her. Her fur was glossier than paraffin.

'The hair-growing lotion you made is a big hit, eh?' Zorba meowed.

'Yeah, I'll let her thank me, then she can leave.'

As she got closer, Pasha, who was wearing a white bolero and beret, rose to her hind legs. 'Floss told me about yesterday's heroics, so I thought I'd better come and make sure…' She stopped meowing, gave me a horrified look and swiped at Zorba. 'I told you to take care of him.'

Pasha's eyes swept up Zorba's fur, as if she didn't recognise the cat standing before her. She hid her confusion by glowering at his bandana. 'I'll have words with you later – you trussed salami,' she

121

meowed, turning to Floss and poking him. 'You were holding something back. Now spit it out or *you* can go elsewhere for your manicures.'

Floss raised a paw to look at his glittery claws, then flapped at his tail with it. 'All I know, ducks,' he meowed, blowing me a kiss, 'is that Captain Omzak's my hero.'

'Enough,' I meowed.

'Enough.' Zorba mimicked my tone of voice.

Pasha tugged her beret down and gave me a furious flash of her eyes. 'Right then, tell me why you look like you've been in a fight with a frying pan.'

I stifled a nervous laugh. 'Listen, Prune Face, I'm not in the mood for this today.'

'Speak,' Pasha meowed.

I pushed her face away from my nose. 'Just *shut up* and sit down. And that means all of you,' I meowed to the others.

The triplets bounced onto their behinds, swishing their tails like windscreen wipers.

Pasha gave Floss a worried look, held his paws and sat next to him.

'What I'm going to say will come as a shock. It came as a big one, even to me.'

'And me! May the saints save us all,' Zorba meowed, making the sign of the cross.

I began with Jodie's dream, what Bongo had said

when he ran back after the party and my decision to do some research. By the time I got to the train station part, Pasha and Floss's paws were tightly clasped.

'When I came to, on the train tracks, I decided to follow the feral cats' scent and found myself at the dried-up lake.' I shook my head, still unable to believe it. 'There, camouflaged with twigs, was Skabbart's spaceship – full of terrified cats.'

Their tails quivering with fright, Pasha and Floss kept their eyes glued on Zorba. He was stomping about, pretending to be an ape that was throwing victims in a sack.

'Skabbart plans to leave tonight,' I meowed, 'which means our work's cut out for us if we're to save those cats.'

I glanced at the triplets. Their faces were all screwed up, like they were nibbling on lemons.

Floss's mouth was squeezed together like he was constipated.

'But we're not scared, are we?' I meowed.

The triplets untangled their tails, which twisted in a sailor's knot. 'Nah,' they meowed. 'We ain't scared.'

'You OK, Floss?' I meowed. His body had gone into a convulsion.

'I'm fine, lovey,' he shrieked.

I tapped my whiskers, thinking how to begin my

pep talk on ants. 'You've probably never looked at an ant and thought of it as a super force,' I meowed, 'but did you know ...' I went on to deliver such a brilliant speech that by the end I'd even convinced myself that what lay ahead was as easy as pie.

It was only when my audience applauded that I was gripped by a moment of doubt. It was all right filling them with courage, but I knew I was endangering their lives. With a simple squeeze of his hand, Skabbart could crush their heads to pomegranate seeds.

I was still shuddering at the image when Pasha came up to me like a timid dormouse. 'Ooh, chuck. I'd never have spoken to you like that if I hadn't thought you were deluded.'

'Yeah, you owe me an apology,' I meowed.

Pasha gave a guilty blink. 'What can I do to help?'

It was one of the most serious days of my life, but I found myself stifling a smile because I'd seen a way to get my own back. 'You can take off your hat, fill it with stones and keep filling it till I tell you to stop,' I told her.

'What kind of stones?' Pasha meowed, looking none too happy with her task.

'Heavy, jagged ones,' I replied.

'Look at her fluffy tail, the shape of her legs at the back,' Zorba commented as Pasha stomped off. '*That* is the mother of my children.' He prodded me. 'I'll name our first son after you.'

I didn't answer. I had far more important things on my mind.

'Let's get started. What's the plan?' the triplets meowed, jiggling on the spot.

'In the next few hours you're going to learn to be so fast you'll be able to do twenty things at once.'

'This is the best day of my life,' Floss shrilled, practising his boxing thrusts.

'And why do we need stones?' Zorba meowed, watching Pasha clamp her teeth round one and drop it in her beret.

'Do you know the story of David and Goliath?'

The cats shook their heads.

'David was a shepherd boy. He found out that Goliath – a six-foot-nine murderer – was terrorising his town. So he decided to do something about it. He wasn't a trained warrior. His job was tending sheep, but he was an ace hunter and could bring down a bird with a single shot from his...'

'Sling?' Zorba meowed.

'Yes. With *one* stone, David hit Goliath right here.' I tapped the middle of my forehead. 'And killed him dead.'

Floss flapped both paws and opened his mouth as if it was the most wondrous story he'd ever heard.

He let out an ear-piercing meow. 'David's mother must have been so *proud*.'

I ignored Floss's hysterics and carried on. 'So, part of your training involves becoming experts in the use of slings. But there's a lot to do before then, so we'll start with a warm-up and do a hundred of these.'

I jumped down on my forepaws, held a handstand position for thirty seconds, flipped over and stood up again.

'Then we'll have ten of these.' I cartwheeled along the grass and back to my starting position. 'Then walking handstands using one paw only.' I demonstrated, lifting my right front paw off the ground as I hopped away on one paw, then swapping paws on my return.

'Got that?' I meowed.

The triplets nodded gleefully, ready to get started. Floss gave an ecstatic meow and twirled on his toes. Zorba, looking like limp lettuce, miserably patted his belly.

'Do what you can,' I meowed. I could see he was concerned about his bulk.

Zorba's eyes frantically searched for Pasha.

She was nowhere to be seen.

'Her job will keep her busy for ages. By the time she notices you, you'll have discovered your talent.'

'By the time she sees me, I will have discovered my talent,' Zorba meowed, turning it over in his mind. 'It's good. I'll make it my new mantra.'

I clasped my paws behind my back. 'Unless I tell you to speak, there's to be no talking.' I walked along my line of recruits. 'And there's to be no slacking – got that?' I bellowed, making them jump in the air.

'Yes, captain!' they saluted.

'So let me see a hundred handstand flips,' I meowed.

For the next three hours, my patience was tested. Big time. The triplets kept crashing into each other like bumper cars because they stuck so close. Floss pirouetted whenever he got flustered, which was most of the time, and Zorba kept landing on his head and knocking himself out.

In short, it was a nightmare. I needed three months to whip them into shape.

Finally, and only because I was such a brilliant trainer, I moved them on from handstands to single paw flips. So much sweat was pouring off them you'd have thought they were in a sauna.

'Stop and watch,' I meowed, to give them a second to cool off.

I cartwheeled again, but this time I included a mid-air body twist.

'Your turn,' I meowed.

The triplets helped each other up. 'Foo, this is hot work,' they meowed.

Floss used Zorba's back to haul himself up, his hind legs more bendy than runner beans.

Zorba's tongue was hanging out. 'Water, water,' he meowed.

'Stop being a sissy and get on with it,' I instructed.

The triplets and Floss mastered the new move in one go.

Zorba tried it and knocked himself out. I left him lying on the grass while I taught the others some self-defence techniques.

'So, having learned joint locks, submission holds, pinning, throwing, punching and kicking, we now have two forms of strike,' I meowed. '*Shomenuchi*, a vertical strike to the head, and *Yokomenuchi*, a lateral strike to the side of the head or neck.'

'What'd he say?' the triplets meowed, giving Floss a poke.

'*Shomenuchi*,' Floss meowed in falsetto. '*Yokomenuchi*,' he shrilled. 'Just saying it gives me goosebumps.'

'Sho-meni-cutsie,' the triplets meowed, struggling to say it.

'Forget it,' I said. 'Just remember one's vertical, slicing down, and the other's lateral, slicing across.'

The triplets and Floss, caught up in their new-found skills, competed against each other through nods to see who could do them best. I saw these, but since they weren't talking or breaking my rules, I let them get on with it. Zorba didn't even try to compete. He had his work cut out keeping up. His tongue lolling out, he delivered a vertical strike to Floss's head.

'*Shomenuchi*,' Floss meowed, striking Zorba back with zeal.

Zorba's eyes boggled and he skidded backwards. 'Not so hard, what's the matter with you?' he meowed.

'And to finish off,' I commanded, 'let me see ten forward flips on your front right paw, then a backward flip on your left.'

The triplets and Floss flipped across the grass.

Zorba bent over, balanced his weight on his front right paw and dangled there, too tired to move.

'Oh, there's Jodie. At ease. Lunch break, men.' I shook my head to remind myself my trainees were Earth cats and not Catopian warriors.

I prodded Zorba in the backside because he was snoring. 'Back on your feet.'

Zorba didn't budge.

'Pasha's coming,' I meowed.

In a second, Zorba was not only upright, he was jogging on the spot like a marathon runner.

25

Jodie joins the Earth cat warriors

Pasha, looking as sweaty as Zorba, dabbed her cheeks with her beret. 'I've collected three piles of stones. Will you be wanting any more?'

'I'll tell you when I've had a look.'

I walked over to Jodie. 'This is Jodie,' I meowed to the assembled cats.

'I brought some extra things I thought you might need,' Jodie said, bringing the shopping trolley she was pushing to a stop. She waved at the cats, who were watching her curiously. 'Hello everybody.'

Spotting Zorba, Jodie went over and knelt down. 'You must be Zorba,' she said, shaking his paw. 'The magnetosphere's really cool, and I love the Minnie Mouse sticker, and…' she brought her mouth to his ear, 'I think you're much better than royalty.'

Zorba licked her face then tapped his paw twice.

'You're very welcome,' Jodie said.

I scratched my ruff. 'You understand him.'

'Sometimes,' Jodie said, giving a tut. 'You should listen when I tell you things.'

'Sorry, I'm out of touch with what goes on in the *normal* world,' I said.

Jodie started giggling. 'You're so funny, Omzak.'

'Give them something to eat,' I said, flicking away a wasp. 'While they're eating I'm going to go and have a quiet think.'

'I brought *you* a ham sandwich and a piece of fudge cake,' she said, laying down a plastic tablecloth. She pulled the tops off four cat food containers. 'For the rest of you there's beef with spinach, lamb with carrots, one with salmon and one with tuna.'

Pasha, who refrained from licking her lips with the others, inched a step forward and gave a sniff.

'I'll be back in an hour,' I said, marching off.

I took a few steps and turned back. 'Zorba, we need to alert every cat in Mapulsbury not to leave their homes tonight. Who can we send?'

'Bongo and his friends,' Zorba meowed, nudging Jodie to share out the food.

'Who can we get as extras to distract Skabbart?'

'Bongo and his friends,' Zorba repeated, watching Jodie pour milk in a dish.

I looked at Pasha, royally waiting for lunch. 'Pasha, go and brief Bongo will you … Tell him to be here with his friends by nine tonight.' I glanced at

131

the piles of stones. 'And be quick because we need more ammunition.'

Pasha's tail banged the grass in anger. Gaining control she turned to Jodie and meowed.

'Does Pasha have to go somewhere?' Jodie asked.

'Yes.' I waved Pasha to get a move on.

'Don't worry, I'll save you yours,' Jodie said, stroking Pasha's head.

Pasha gave Jodie's wrist a lick and sauntered off. As soon as she cleared the first tree, she started running like a greyhound.

26

All for one and one for all

When I returned from my think, Pasha was back and there were six huge piles of stones. I suspected she'd enlisted help but as long as the job was done, I didn't care.

Lunch had been eaten and cleared away. Jodie was telling the cats the story of Dick Whittington. I assumed she's chosen that one because Dick's cat played a part in it.

Zorba's head was squeezed under her arm. He kept nudging her to rub his ears. Nearby, Pasha stared into space, as if the tale was childish. But whenever Jodie used words like riches and royalty, her ears pricked up like matchsticks.

'And so Dick Whittington ran away from the mansion he'd been working in because the cook there was so mean to him,' Jodie said, tickling Zorba's chin.

'Dick only had one penny and he used it to buy a cat. He called him Puss and they travelled everywhere together. It turned out Puss was a brilliant mouse catcher … and … can you guess what happened next?'

The triplets looked at each other then at the ground.

'A famous king asked Dick if he could have Puss,' Jodie continued, 'because his palace was overrun with mice.

'And the king was so grateful, he rewarded Dick with a treasure chest, making him very wealthy,' I interrupted. I clapped my paws to get everyone's attention. 'Story time over. We've got work to do.'

Jodie moaned. 'But I haven't told them how Dick Whittington became Mayor of London yet.'

'If they're that interested they can read the story for themselves.'

'He looked at Jodie and pointed to a hefty oak. 'Put what you've brought under that tree – and bring your pad. I've thought of more things we need.'

'Hold on a mo',' the triplets meowed, squashing themselves on Jodie's lap. Their ginger striped tails curled like liquorice wheels and they tapped her chest. 'Meeow, murr, miaaaaow.'

'Sorry, I didn't get all that,' Jodie said. She looked at me. 'What did the triplets say?'

'That you're peculiar enough to join Le Freak – that's the name of their gang.'

'I'd love to,' Jodie said.

Zorba extracted his head from under Jodie's arm, twitched his nose and ran a paw down his ear.

'Zorba says I can't.'

'Why?'

Zorba headbutted Jodie's arm. 'He says only if you join.'

The triplets jumped off Jodie's lap and went down on their paws to beg like dogs. 'Please guv, do us this honour?'

'Join us, chuck – go on. It'll be another thing to add to your memoirs,' Pasha meowed, giving her chest a queenly lick.

'I should have known you were a member,' I meowed at her.

'You didn't think all Earth cats were like us, did you?' She patted her ruby collar. 'We're the *crème de la crème* – the best of the best.' She glanced at Zorba, who was putting his bandana back on. 'And those who aren't, have extra special talents – like inventing.'

'I have many talents,' Zorba meowed, jumping to his feet. He picked a bluebell and held it out. 'Maybe you'd like to walk with me tomorrow?' he asked Pasha.

Jodie shook the tip of Zorba's tail to prod him closer.

'If you're around tomorrow, we'll see, you big daft

lump,' Pasha meowed, taking the flower. She looked teary. *Is Zorba winning her over?*

Jodie poked me in the side. 'Please, let's join Le Freak,' she said.

The triplets were beseeching me with their eyes. I still couldn't tell who was who without checking out their tails.

Floss stroked his combat jacket. 'We'd be united, even after death, lovey.'

The word 'death' hit me like a meteorite collision. *Will they come out of the battle alive?* Strange as it was, I'd grown attached to these crazy cats. 'Oh, all right,' I meowed.

Jodie held out her hand and grinned. 'High five!'

I tapped her palm with my paw. 'High five.'

The cats gathered round to see what we were doing.

'Put your paws on top of my hand,' she told them.

Zorba went first, then Pasha, then the triplets, then Floss.

'Put your paw on top now,' she instructed me.

'I hope this isn't going to take long, we've got ...'

Jodie grabbed my paw with her spare hand, put it on top of the pile and closed her eyes. 'We, the members of Le Freak, promise to always be friends, never let anyone bully us ...'

Floss let out a shrill meow. '*Never* let anyone bully us.'

'Never be arrogant,' Jodie continued, 'and save any cats that need rescuing.' She hesitated. 'Erm … Amen.'

'Mee-em,' chorused the cats.

'Good, now no more interruptions,' I meowed, marching towards the oak.

Jodie wheeled the trolley over, took a plastic box out of a bag and handed it to me. 'This is your lunch.'

'I'd almost forgotten,' I said, taking a few quick bites of my sandwich.

'What do I write on my list?' Jodie asked.

Zorba, paws clasped behind his back, as he'd seen me do, tapped her shin with his nose, opened his mouth and made panting sounds.

'Water,' Jodie wrote.

I took a swig of orange juice to help the sandwich go down and swallowed. 'Have you got any ping-pong balls?'

Jodie nodded. 'In our shed.'

'Bring the lot – and a roll of tin foil, a pen and a box of matches.'

'And matches,' Jodie wrote. She blew the fringe from her eyes.

I gave my whiskers a twirl. 'That's it – now, back to work,' I ordered the cats.

Jodie closed her pad and brushed some grass bits off her jeans. 'I'll be back quick as I can.'

27

Will smoke bombs be enough?

I watched my little army swinging through the trees with the ease of monkeys. Hanging on by one paw, they jumped to another branch.

'Stand and fire!' I meowed.

They rose up on their hind legs. With the slings gripped in one front paw, they used the free one to load another stone from their pouches. *Ping. Ping. Ping. Ping*

The round of stones hit the chalk circles that had been drawn on the trunk of a nearby elm.

'Bullseye,' Zorba meowed, hitting the cherry-sized dot in the middle. I nodded with pride. The last runner in the race *had* found his talent.

'That makes ninety-three.' Zorba glanced at Pasha and gave her a cheeky wink. He turned to me and mouthed, 'My mantra was a good one, eh?'

'Well, you've proved you're a great slingshot,' I meowed, waving the cats to come down out of the tree.

'I'm back,' Jodie shouted, wearing a denim jacket because of the chill in the air. She shook a flask at me. 'Would you like a cup of tea?'

'Maybe later. Did you find everything?'

Jodie nodded, pulled her hood over her head and sat down on the grass. She opened her jacket. 'It's got fleecy lining,' she said to Pasha. 'We can share if you want.'

Pasha daintily shook out her paws and snuggled next to Jodie.

'One last thing and we'll call it a day.' I pointed to a roll of wire netting I'd attached to a long, thick branch. 'Triplets, one of your jobs tonight is to secure it to the roof of the hut, then, when I give the signal, you're to drop it.'

The triplets climbed the tree. 'Stand in position along the trunk.' I raised a paw. 'Untie and drop.'

The first attempt took them twenty seconds and the ninth attempt took fourteen. By the time they'd done it fifty times, they'd improved, but were running out of steam. 'Two seconds. Good enough,' I meowed. 'Now take it down. The rest of you can gather the stones you fired and put everything in a heap.'

On hearing this, Pasha extracted herself from Jodie's coat and went over to Zorba. 'Might as well make myself useful,' she meowed, patting a stone his way.

When I marched over to Jodie, she was sitting with her knees hugged in to her chest. 'I'm glad Pasha changed her mind about wanting a cat with a royal title,' she said, breaking into giggles. 'Look how cute Zorba is.'

I turned to look. Zorba, using his tail like a cricket bat, was cockily whacking stones into her beret.

'Yep, he's a klutz,' I said. 'Let's get to it. We've got smoke bombs to make.'

'Is that why you wanted the ping-pong balls and stuff?' Jodie asked.

I nodded. 'Get it all out and rip the foil into ten strips.'

When Jodie finished, I placed three balls in the first and crumpled it in a loose parcel. I moulded the foil round a pen, then took it out and blew down the hole. Watching carefully, Jodie copied me.

'What does sticking a pen into them do?' she said, blowing into the last package.

'Gives the smoke somewhere to escape when we light them,' I said.

I looked up at the sky. From the setting sun I guessed the time was close to nine. In the distance, I could see Bongo and his friends running down a hill towards me.

A sickly feeling came over me. My tail nervously swept the ground. Smoke bombs, ropes and the rest weren't enough against Skabbart's high-tech weapons. And the worst part was, I had to take him back alive.

'Are you all right, Omzak? Your whiskers are jerking,' Jodie said.

'Yeah, yeah,' I said. I smacked my tail to stop it swishing. 'Collect everything, put it in the trolley, then put the smoke bombs on top – and remember what I told you. You're to do as you're told and not to go anywhere near Skabbart,' I added, wishing I hadn't been bribed into letting her come.

28

Everyone's got the shakes

'So repeat what you said so we don't make any mistakes,' Bongo meowed, his whiskers quivering.

I looked at the two friends he'd brought along. One's eyes had frozen like he'd gone into a trance. The other was scratching a nervous hole in the earth.

'First of all,' I meowed, 'the three of you need to calm down. Skabbart's vicious but he's not twenty foot tall, his fangs aren't made of razor blades and he doesn't breathe fire like a dragon.'

'What about his talons?' one of the friends piped up. 'We heard that with one squeeze our guts will spew out of our mouths.'

'Make sure you don't get close enough to find out,' I meowed.

Jodie was pushing the stacked trolley towards me. Zorba, Floss and the triplets were marching by her side.

I glanced at Bongo and his friends, who still

looked like nervous wrecks. 'Take courage from them,' I meowed.

'Yeah,' Bongo said, struggling to sound brave. He washed his ears then lengthened his neck. 'So what you said was, we're to go to the hut, pretend we were just passing by, and when Skabbart and his accomplice come out, we're to make a run for it?'

I nodded. 'Yep.'

'Then we have to divert them, to give you five minutes to fix everything, and lure them back again.'

'Right,' I meowed. I knew they'd probably be in Skabbart's sack by this point, but telling them wouldn't help.

The wind gave a low howl and the moon disappeared behind a thick band of clouds. 'Time to move out,' I meowed, hoping we'd be around to see the sun rise.

29

Will we come out of this battle alive?

Without warning, the sky turned black as coal. A streak of lightning crackled across it. The bottom fell out of a heavy cloud. It wasn't long before the earth was a squelchy swamp and our paws were sucked into the mud.

For a while, the howl of the windy storm drowned out any other sound. Leaves slapped us in the face as they swirled by. Trees shook like menacing trolls. It felt as if invisible eyes were watching our every move.

Marching single file behind me was Zorba, then Floss, then the triplets. Bringing up the rear was Jodie. Occasionally, when the wind dropped, I heard the rattle of the trolley as she manoeuvred it over a bumpy patch. Or the crack of bracken under her feet.

Something growled behind a bush. A fox came out and bared its teeth. 'Don't even dream it.' I struck it with a stick. It plunged into the under-growth.

Just then Zorba slid and crashed into my back. 'Ooh, sorry,' he meowed, blasting me with his steaming breath.

I watched an owl swoop down and clamp a mouse in its claws. Its terrified squeaks gave me the shivers. *Was I right to involve Zorba and his friends in this battle? What if I can't protect them?*

I glanced up at the smudgy moon breaking through the clouds. The rain had stopped as suddenly as it started. 'The spaceship's that way,' I meowed.

Zorba wrung out his bandana and put it back on. 'Tell us one last time what we have to do.'

'As soon as we get there,' I meowed, 'you'll tie the ropes to the tree.'

'And then,' the triplets meowed, shaking their bodies and splattering me with raindrops, 'we're to secure the netting to the roof.'

'Quick as you can,' I meowed, shaking the water out of my coat.

Jodie, feet squeaking in the mud, pulled up beside me. Her fringe was dripping with rain. 'And you're to stay hidden behind a tree and only if and when I signal ...'

'... am I to come out,' Jodie finished my sentence, shivering.

'Don't forget that – I mean it.'

I turned to Floss. I could hear trickling water. His

pink face had turned the colour of a raspberry. 'I'll never forgive myself,' he meowed, stepping out of his self-made puddle.

Jodie handed him the hankie she'd blown her nose with. 'Here you are, Floss,' she said.

'Even the fiercest warriors have bladder problems,' I meowed, watching him dab his legs.

He gave his combat jacket a tug. 'That's right, Captain Omzak.' He flapped a paw. 'Inside, I'm the fiercest warrior you've ever met.'

'One last reminder of the signals, then,' I meowed. 'When I hoot like an owl, release the netting. When I howl like a wolf, get on your ropes and attack Skabbart from above.' I gave my soggy whiskers a twirl. 'And remember – one mistake and we're done for.'

The stink of rotting meat knocked me sideways. 'Skabbart and his accomplice have left the hut,' I meowed, my heart thumping in my mouth. 'Let's do it.'

30

Facing up to Skabbart

'Don't listen to the howls coming through the walls of the spaceship,' I meowed as we approached. The spaceship rattled as the kidnapped cats threw themselves at the door.

'I hope my Uncle Tickles hasn't been squashed,' Zorba murmured.

'Whatever you do, don't go near the ship,' I ordered. 'If you alert the hostages, they'll start yowling even more and Skabbart will get suspicious.'

'No. I was just saying,' Zorba meowed, rubbing mud off his tail.

'Wait here while I check the coast is clear,' I instructed, going ahead to the hut. The door was open. The Varians weren't inside, but their stink clung to every corner. 'Unpack the trolley,' I called out.

'Straight away, Captain Omzak,' Jodie said, putting everything on the ground.

I signalled to the cats and pointed to the tree they were to climb.

Zorba bit into a length of rope, stuck his claws in the trunk and climbed up. He knotted the rope around a stump, came back down and started again.

I glanced at the triplets. Then at Floss. Between them they'd tied three.

Jodie was watching them, fascinated. 'Why are they doing that?'

'So they can swing on them and pelt stones from a height. It might be useful if … I jabbed Jodie's shin. 'What are you still doing here? Go and hide,' I whispered.

Jodie crossed her fingers. 'Good luck, Omzak.'

Holding my breath, I went in the hut. Hanging on the wall was a metal ball zoomifier. The weapon was powerful enough to blast a hole through an elephant. I rattled the chains securing it then thumped the lock with my fists. With time on my side, I could have smashed it off. But I didn't have time and there wasn't a key.

Outside I could hear the triplets nailing the netting to the roof and the whispered meows of Zorba and Floss.

CRUNCH, CRUNCH, CRUNCH. My ears pricked up. I heard a crackle of twigs and the thud of feet.

'Quick, hide in that ditch,' I meowed, my mouth dryer than a sand dune.

Hot on my tail the other cats followed. We dived into its muddy banks. Not long after, Skabbart appeared, clumping the way he did. Gangly arms swinging. Tail sweeping the mud.

Floss let out a squeak of terror. 'His teeth are like vampire fa ...'

I clapped a paw over his mouth.

'His eyes are like purple cockroaches!' the triplets gasped.

'Ssh!' I jogged them.

'Po, Po. Po, may the saints save us,' Zorba quaked. 'His tail is thicker than a dinosaur.'

'Shut up!' I meowed.

Terror ran through my blood. Not for me. For them. *If they have the guts to go through with it, will they come out alive?*

Dimp came into view. He had a sack over his shoulder. Inside, Bongo and his friends squirmed like eels.

'They've got them,' Zorba meowed, giving a nervous belch.

'Shut up,' I repeated. 'You'll blow our cover.'

Skabbart stared into the forest, his ears splayed out like a deer's.

We ducked our heads so he didn't spot us.

'Did you just hear a cat meow?' Skabbart asked Dimp.

Luckily, Bongo and his friends were howling. 'These three, I expect.' Dimp threw the sack on the ground. 'You should have used your stun pistol on them, Captain.'

'Puh, they were sitting with their paws up in surrender,' Skabbart sneered.

I peered over the ditch to see what was going on.

'I'm sick of this miserable place,' Skabbart said, spitting out a lump of phlegm.

Dimp looked down at the sack. 'Shall I throw these in the spaceship with the others?'

'No, bring them inside the hut,' Skabbart said. 'They can't get out. Let's pack up and go.'

31

A battle like no other

'Smoke bombs,' I meowed to Zorba. I rubbed at my
fur to get the mud off. It spread like peanut butter.
'Triplets – get up on the roof and wait for my signal.
Floss, stand by.'

Zorba and I carried the smoke bombs to the door.
I lit a match, held it against the first bomb and kept
going. Streaks of smoke came out of the funnels.
Zorba coughed and shielded his eyes.

'As soon as I break the door down, start
throwing.' I ran at it and rammed it with my head.
It fell apart like rice paper. Within seconds Zorba
had torpedoed the hut.

'I told you those three cats were sent as spies,'
Skabbart spluttered. He thumped his gorilla fists on
the table. The stun pistol clattered to the floor.

I kicked it out of hut, went back in and tugged the
sack towards the door.

'Where's that sack?' Skabbart coughed. 'I'm going
to chop off their heads and impale them on spikes –

to teach their meddling friends a lesson.' His voice was muffled, as if he was talking through his hand. 'Where are you, you idiot?'

'Looking for the sack,' Dimp said.

I heard a crack as their heads met. Then the sound of a hefty slap.

'Find me the torch, you useless dimwit!' Skabbart screamed.

Biting my whiskers so I wouldn't cough, I dragged the sack out of the hut and dropped it in front of Zorba.

'Let them out, I'm going back in,' I meowed to him. I tugged off his bandana and tied it round my mouth.

Skabbart was bent over, wheezing. 'Give me the torch!' he yelled. 'I need to unlock the zoomifier.' I could hear keys jangling. I leapt at Skabbart's waist belt and tried to yank it off him. The studs were too tight. My paws were clammy. SNAP. I prised one open.

Talons ripped into my neck. A bolt of pain shot out of my ears. I looked up to see a torch shining in my face.

'It's a cat bandit,' Skabbart screamed, pulling me off.

I backflipped, knocked the torch from Dimp's hand, ran to the door and tossed it in the ditch.

'Where's my stun gun?' Skabbart shouted. 'Get him, get him!'

Skabbart and Dimp clumped outside. The tufts of hair on top of their heads stuck out like spiky helmets. There was still so much smog, Skabbart couldn't see us.

I hooted like an owl.

The netting came down to trap Skabbart and Dimp. I caught the bottom and pulled it out. Zorba nailed it in the earth.

I howled like a wolf.

The triplets flew through the air and grabbed their ropes with one front paw. They used the other to pelt stones at Skabbart.

'You pesky vermin,' Skabbart spluttered, as stone after stone bounced off him.

There was a ripping sound. Dimp's hand came through the netting. 'Got you!' he said, swinging Floss by his tail.

Listening to Floss's squeals as he was smacked against the hut, I grabbed the stun pistol and fired a round of shots. I knew they wouldn't do much damage. The pellets weren't strong enough to bring down a Varian. But they made him rattle like a skeleton, giving Floss the chance to fight back. He twirled in a cocoon, socked Dimp's face with all four paws then sank his claws in his neck.

'We have become good, eh?' Zorba meowed, hammering a nail in Skabbart's tail.

Skabbart howled like a coyote. 'As soon as I get

out of here,' he bellowed as he yanked his tail free, 'I'm going to skin you and turn you into hats.' He jumped up and down, shaking the netting.

'Time to do a bit of damage.' I aimed my sling at Skabbart's nose.

'Aarrrggh!' His nose spurted with blood. Using his fangs like scissors, he started cutting through the wire.

'Cover me, Zorba.' I passed him the sling, climbed up the netting, forced the other studs of Skabbart's belt undone and jumped to the ground with it. 'Get this to Jodie for safekeeping,' I meowed to Zorba.

'RUHHH!' Skabbart growled. He pushed his shoulders through the cut wires. He tugged at the netting. And kept tugging.

CR-AAACK. A plank fell off the roof. The netting collapsed in a heap over Skabbart's head.

He threw it off and peered down at me with murder in his eyes. I knew he hadn't recognised me because I wasn't wearing my military jacket. And my fur was brown with mud instead of white.

'So, we meet again, scumbag,' I twirled my whiskers to remind him who I was.

Skabbart's mouth foamed up. 'I should have known you were behind this, you snivelling buzzard excrement!' His hand flew to his waist.

'You won't find it.' I threw him a stick. 'We're fighting fair and square.'

Skabbart caught it and flung it back. His tail slashed round and whipped my face. 'Fair and square, you lump of dung????' He lunged at me with his talons.

I dodged under his legs.

Using his hairy clumps of fur as a ladder, I raced up Skabbart's back, locked my paws round his neck and squeezed. 'Give in, before there's bloodshed.'

Skabbart bounced up and down. 'I *love* blood.' He rolled over, pinned my arms down and opened his foul-smelling mouth.

I drew my hind legs up, kicked him in the gut and slid out from underneath. 'OK, we'll do it your way.'

Skabbart's tail shot up. I grabbed the end of it and rode it like a cowboy. 'GRRRRR, GRRRRR.' Skabbart turned in circles, trying to grab me.

PING. A nail went in his snout. PING. Another in his arm. I glanced up to see Zorba. He was standing on a branch firing nails from his sling.

'Arrrrgh!' Skabbart screamed. He toppled back and slammed into the hut. It flattened like a cardboard box.

There was so much going on I couldn't take it in: cats flying on ropes, cats cartwheeling past, Floss catapulting over Dimp's head.

I flew at Skabbart and kicked him in the stomach. Down he went in a mountain of dust. He bounced to his feet and charged me, talons out, ready to kill.

I whirled in mid-air.

Using the side of my paw, I struck his head, first with a knife hand – BOOF! – then with a hammer fist – BOOF! BOOF! We rolled in a heap and Skabbart punched my face. I winced as red-hot pain shot through my skull. My mouth filled with blood. It dribbled down my chin.

I jammed a forepaw under his chin and pressed down on his neck, squashing his windpipe. 'Give up.'

Skabbart gripped hold of my whiskers and tugged. I could hear them tearing out at the roots. It was worse than being pricked with a thousand needles. My paw slipped off his windpipe.

'I've had enough,' Skabbart snarled, tossing me to the ground. 'It's extermination time.'

Dimp had given up. He was lying in the rubble, waving a cloth.

I leapt to my feet and neatly dodged Skabbart. 'Triplets, I need to get the zoomifier before Skabbart,' I meowed as I zipped past them. 'Do something to waylay him.'

'Right, guv.' They somersaulted onto Skabbart's back and clung on like leeches.

'Get off, you vermin,' Skabbart screeched.

With Zorba at my side, we loosened the fallen planks of the hut and started dragging the zoomifier out.

Skabbart had rolled on his back. He was bouncing up and down on the triplets. 'Let's see how you like this,' he said. There was the crack of breaking bones.

'If you're OK, I'll go save the triplets,' Zorba meowed.

'Jump to it.' I gripped the zoomifier with all four paws. It was wedged under something. It wouldn't shift.

'Think of the mightiness of ants,' Floss shrilled, wrapping his forepaws round my middle. Together we yanked it out. As we did, something whacked us on the head.

I heard a falsetto meow as Floss passed out. I shook the spots from my eyes to see ... *Skabbart* standing over me.

'The End.' Skabbart sneered, pointing the zoomifier at my head. 'I was going to keep you as my slave, but I'll have more fun watching your eyeballs explode.'

'Once a scumbag, always a scumbag,' I said, holding my breath. The smell coming out of his mouth was vile.

'We aren't all fortunate enough to be famous Catopian warriors.' Skabbart's eyes looked as if they were brimming with tears. 'Do you know what it's like when all you've heard since you've grown your first fang is, "Skabbart's useless. Skabbart will never amount to anything. Skabbart's so ugly we can't look at him."?' He rested a finger on the trigger. 'Goodbye you…'

I leapt at his feet and ripped out a claw. The earth beneath me exploded.

FOOM, PZZZ, BAM. Metal balls shot out of the zoomifier, setting everything they touched alight. Within seconds there was a path of scorched grass across the forest floor. Flames whipped through the shrubs like gremlins. I could smell singeing hair. I touched my mouth. MY WHISKERS WERE ON FIRE!

I patted the stubble frantically until the flames went out. 'You've done it now.' I flew at Skabbart, knocking the zoomifier from his grasp with a mid-air kick.

Zorba and Floss pounced on it. Floss held it up while Zorba took aim.

Skabbart gave me a sickly smile. 'Let's talk about this. I've made a serum that can turn anyone into our slaves. We can rule Catopia together. We can rule every planet in every galaxy.'

'Listen, snot bag. You're everything I hate. I'd like nothing better than to finish you off – but I'm taking you back alive, to let your own kind deal with you.'

Skabbart lurched towards me. 'That's what you think, you whiskerless lump of snot.'

Fury ripped through me like a house on fire. I got Skabbart in a stranglehold and pummelled him with my back paws. 'You shouldn't have reminded me about my whiskers.' His eyes had glassed over. I went on pummelling.

'Stop,' Jodie said, climbing over the rubble.

'Get out, get away!' I screamed.

'I saw flames,' Jodie said, looking Skabbart up and down.

His hand jerked out to grab her. 'My road to freedom. You're coming with me, little girl.'

Jodie jumped back and snarled like an angry dog. 'I'm not scared of you.' She whacked Skabbart over the head with a plank. 'You stole my cat, you horrible Varian.'

A stone from Zorba's sling lodged between Skabbart's eyes. 'I would have made it go through his brain but I'm following your rules,' Zorba meowed.

'Aaaaargh!' Skabbart screeched. 'Take it out, I'm going blind.'

I punched Skabbart on the nose, knocking him out. I removed the stone. 'Quick, let's bind him before he comes to,' I ordered Zorba and Floss.

While they worked on Skabbart's feet, I made sure his hands were tied together tight.

'What happened to Bongo and his friends?' I meowed.

'They got scared when they heard Skabbart threaten to impale their heads on spikes,' Zorba said with a grin.

'The triplets?'

'They cracked a few ribs. They are sitting by the tree resting.' Zorba meowed.

'On the whole, we got off lightly.'

'Apart from this,' Zorba gestured to the scorch mark running down the middle of his body. He nodded at Floss. 'And Floss's black eyes.' Zorba looked at my whiskers and meowed with laughter. 'You know how funny you look without your whiskers?'

'Don't remind me.' I gave Skabbart a kick.

Jodie was bent over Dimp. One of the cats must have hit him. He was out cold. Jodie was examining him like a detective.

'Move away from him,' I yelled.

'Varians stink, their fingers look like smoked sausages, their fangs are full of cracks and their ears look like bat's wings,' Jodie said.

'If you haven't got a camera to take a picture, go and get Skabbart's belt,' I said, holding Skabbart down.

Jodie clambered over the rubble. 'I can't believe what that weapon did to the forest. It's still smouldering,' she said.

'You'll be the one smouldering in a minute. Go and do what I asked,' I said.

Jodie clapped her hands together. 'Oh, goody, we're going to release Horacio.'

32

A cat wedding and sad goodbyes

When I opened the spaceship door, it was like watching water gush out of a dam. Trampling on each other, or clinging to each other's backs, the trapped cats scattered out into the forest. I saw Horacio jump into Jodie's arms and Zorba hugging a cat I guessed was his Uncle Tickles. The rest was a blur of fur, until the last tail disappeared over the horizon.

Skabbart and his accomplice were out cold, and looked like they'd stay that way. I tied Zorba's bandana round Skabbart's mouth, to stop him ranting when he came round.

When I glanced up, the triplets were limping towards me. 'Did we bind Skabbart's accomplice with enough rope, guv?' they meowed.

'He'd have to be Houdini to get out of that.'

'Whodidni?' the triplets chirruped, clutching at their sides in pain.

'Houdini was famous for escaping from things,' I meowed. 'By the way, thanks for your help. Jodie can take you back on the trolley.'

The triplets hopped forwards, supporting each other.

'That battle was amazing, guv,' they meowed. 'Who'd have thought ordinary cats like us would have been involved in bringing down a villain from another galaxy.' Their eyes turned to light gold with the joy of their achievement.

'Let's hope you'll use what you've learned to help others defend themselves,' I said.

'Zorba's already organised it, guv. He doesn't want his kittens to grow up in fear. He's planning on having six.'

'Six? That should keep him busy,' I grinned.

The triplets glanced around, like they were looking for someone. 'We're all here except Jodie. Where is she?'

'Hosing down the spaceship to get rid of the stink,' I meowed, as Jodie came out, soaked from head to foot.

'All done.' Jodie announced, sneezing as she skipped towards me.

'As soon as you get home, I want you to put your magnetosphere on,' I said.

She jiggled her wrist. 'I haven't taken it off, so I'm invincible.' Jodie laughed and bent down to stroke the triplets. 'Hi, members of Le Freak.'

'Mee ar, meeoo,' the triplets chimed, sticking out their left legs.

'Aw, you've hurt yourselves,' Jodie said. 'When we get back I'll take you to the vet's right away.'

I turned to watch Zorba and Floss drag Skabbart's accomplice over the grass.

'You two hold one foot and I'll grab the other,' I meowed, joining them. 'On the count of three – pull!'

Once inside the spaceship, I familiarised myself with the control panel while Zorba and Floss looked on in wonder.

'Ooh, what I wouldn't give to have one of these,' Floss meowed. 'With pink walls and pink leather sofas.'

'And I could say to Pasha: "How would you like to come for a spin in my spaceship?"' Zorba meowed.

I tapped out my message to Leorio. *On my way home, sir. Have Skabbart and accomplice on-board.*

Zorba slapped a paw on my shoulder. 'If you're writing to your ruler, I would like to …'

I pressed *send*. 'I'll give him your regards when I get back.'

Zorba pinched my cheek. 'I will miss you, my friend.'

'Just because I didn't shirk your paw off, doesn't mean you can take liberties,' I said.

When we came out, Jodie was tugging Skabbart to the spaceship.

'What d'you think you're up to?'

'I'm doing this for Horacio, for when I tell him the story,' Jodie said.

I grabbed Skabbart's head and pushed with her. 'Well, don't go breaking any fingers – or you won't be able to play at the Pavilion.'

'I wish you could be there on my big night,' Jodie said, as we tossed Skabbart in the ship. 'But I know you've got to go back to Catopia – to be a leader for others.'

'You'll be amazing,' I said. I went to twirl my whiskers.

'You're even more handsome without your whiskers, Omzak,' Jodie said.

'I feel naked.' I ran my paws over the stubble.

'You don't look arrogant any more.'

I studied Jodie's face. Her cheeks were flushed from excitement. Her eyes looked softer. 'You don't either.'

Jodie nodded. 'My dad said he's glad I've forgiven him. He's coming to the concert.'

'That's great.' I set to washing myself in a puddle of water. I looked up to see Pasha running towards us.

Zorba was rubbing his fur with leaves and hadn't noticed.

'Someone's come to see you,' I meowed.

Pasha stopped in front of Zorba. She gave his face

a lick. 'I suppose we should be thankful yur only injury is a scorch mark. And a bald tail, and a burned nose.'

She gave me one of her Prune Face smiles. 'Fancy you shaving off your whiskers, chuck.'

'Did it specially for you.' I could hear Zorba laugh in the background.

Pasha sidled up to me. 'You've changed all our lives, chuck. We'll never forget you,' she meowed.

Zorba threw his paws around my neck. 'You know how much I love you. Maybe you could marry us before you leave?'

'What did Zorba say?' Jodie asked.

'He wants me to give them my blessing.'

'Ooh, a wedding – wait, we need a bouquet,' Jodie said, running off to pick some flowers.

'Can I be the bridesmaid?' Floss shrilled, giving an excited twirl.

'Course you can, chuck,' Pasha meowed.

'And don't you start crying, eh?' Zorba blubbed.

'You daft lump.' Pasha took the bouquet from Jodie and stood next to Floss. He smoothed down Pasha's cape, purring in song.

'This is so cool,' Jodie said, sitting down on the grass. 'I've never been to a cat wedding before.'

'I've never given a blessing before,' I said.

I glanced up at the sky. The first signs of morning were breaking through. The red of the burnt path was turning yellow. Birds were chirping good mornings. The air smelled of coconut. I sniffed, knowing this was the last smell I'd take with me … And the last time I'd see Zorba.

'In honour of my ancestors,' I meowed, clearing my throat, 'I give this blessing to … my best friend and brother, Zorba, and Pasha, his bride. May you be happy, have long, healthy lives and everything else you want.'

The triplets shook Zorba's tail with theirs. 'Congratulations, Zorb.'

Zorba looked at me and wiped the tears from his eyes. 'Remember, our first son will have your name, eh?'

'It'd be an honour,' I said.

'Kiss the bride, kiss the bride,' Floss meowed, running to catch Pasha's bouquet.

Jodie bent down. 'Let's not say goodbye, Omzak. Let's do this instead.' She held her hand up.

'This has been an amazing experience' I said, gulping back the lump in my throat.

Jodie nodded. 'The best.'

I put my paw in her hand and left it there. 'High five, Jodie.'